The Eye of Ne

A Pharaoh's Cat Novel

Maria Luisa Lang

THE EYE OF NEFERTITI
SEQUEL TO THE PHARAOH'S CAT
Copyright © 2016 by Maria Luisa Lang

Author photo courtesy of Priscilla Brewster

ISBN 978-0-9963352-1-8

For Priscilla

Chapter 1

It's summer, and I'm stretched out on a windowsill in my bedroom with the sunlight warming the fur on my back. It's quiet except for the drone of traffic on the Henry Hudson Parkway and the occasional whir of a helicopter flying along the river.

I once shared this bedroom with my friend Gato-Hamen, the High Priest of Amun-Ra. He and I had fled ancient Egypt on his magic boat. It was only supposed to carry us to a foreign land, but it took us through time as well as space here to Elena's house in twenty-first century New York City.

Elena's late father had been a renowned Egyptologist, and she immediately recognized us as ancient Egyptians. She was surprised we were speaking English. We explained that the prayer which had launched the magic boat also gave us the power to speak the language wherever we arrived.

She was also surprised that I, a cat, could talk and walk like a man. That would be explained later. Overjoyed at the prospect of excitement in her life, she invited us to stay with her.

Now the High Priest shares her bedroom, and I share this one with their child, who's the reincarnation of the Pharaoh I loved thousands of years ago. He's on the floor, playing contentedly with his building blocks. It's hard to believe he's already a year old.

Elena is reading and keeping an eye on him. "Wrappa-Hamen, are you recharging?" she asks, as she always does when she sees me basking in the sun. "You lazy old cat!"

"Lazy, yes. Old, not yet," I reply, too drowsy to say more.

When I first met the Pharaoh, he was sixteen, and I was a stray tomcat. I'd wandered into in a looted tomb and was kicked by the Vizier, his uncle. I spat a cat amulet at him, hitting him on the forehead. He accused me of trying to kill him. The High Priest arrived and tried to reason with him.

Then it happened. I suddenly had human powers! I stood upright, walked over to the Vizier, and debated with him. The Pharaoh entered the tomb to hear me wise-cracking and laughed for the first time since his parents' death. He took me to live with him at court, and we became inseparable.

A year later the Vizier poisoned him and accused me of the

1

murder. He was going to put me to death when the High Priest rescued me. We fled Egypt on the magic boat and ended up in Elena's living room . . .

One night, two weeks after our arrival, the High Priest and I were talking about our despair over the loss of our beloved Pharaoh when Elena suddenly recalled a memory from her childhood. On the night her mother died she'd witnessed her father standing over the body and reading aloud in a foreign language from a piece of yellow paper.

She realized now that the paper had been a papyrus, and that her father had been reading an ancient Egyptian spell to revive the dead in an attempt to save her mother. The High Priest believed that the spell had failed because not even an Egyptologist would know how to pronounce ancient Egyptian correctly—and that if we unearthed the Pharaoh's mummy and he recited the spell, the Pharaoh might be resurrected.

But we couldn't find the papyrus!

That would've been the end of it if the High Priest hadn't remembered a ritual called the Entering which would enable him to place himself inside Elena's memory and listen to her father reciting the spell.

I again feel my relief when the High Priest retrieved the spell.

He then composed a new prayer to launch the magic boat so we could return to Egypt and resurrect the Pharaoh.

I again feel my pain when we left Elena. In the two weeks we'd spent with her, we'd come to love her.

Back in Egypt, we learned that the Vizier had usurped the throne and now ruled as a tyrant. We eventually made our way to the Pharaoh's tomb and removed his mummy from the sarcophagus. The High Priest recited the spell, but nothing happened . . . until the cat-goddess Bastet, who had given me my human powers, appeared and said that for the spell to work I had to be willing to give my life for the Pharaoh's.

Yes! I cried. But I didn't die. Bastet only wanted to see if I could love a man more than myself.

I again feel my joy as the Pharaoh was resurrected, and my terrible pain when, having killed the Vizier in battle, he returned to the world above.

The High Priest, with me at his side, tried to govern Egypt in the Pharaoh's place, but the Vizier's former allies were too powerful. Finally, we had to go into hiding to avoid being killed.

But that's all ancient history now, literally.

The High Priest and I used the magic boat to return to Elena, who told us she was carrying the High Priest's child. I knew immediately that the child was the reincarnation of the Pharaoh I'd loved. I could smell his odor, like the blue lotus, coming from her womb.

Elena and the High Priest soon got used to the idea that their unborn baby was the Pharaoh. The High Priest wanted a name for him which would reflect the Pharaoh's past. "Son of the Sun," "True of Heart," or "Speaker of Truth." Elena had other ideas. "George," "James," or "Stephen." No one asked my opinion.

Elena and the High Priest finally agreed on "Alexander." She was pleased because it was her father's name. He was pleased because the most famous "Alexander" was called "the Great." Because I hadn't been consulted, I didn't tell them I approved.

Alexander was born, the Pharaoh reborn, and Elena, the High Priest, Alexander, and I are a happy family . . .

I hear the little Pharaoh cry and look down at the floor. He's disappeared! I jump down and rush out of the bedroom to find him. He's standing in the middle of the landing, his legs wide apart, his diapers hanging heavy under him. Elena has started toilet training him, but on occasion he has a relapse. It's hard to accept that the little one with full diapers was once a tall, strong, handsome king.

Elena has also come out of the bedroom and is standing between us. "Wrappa-Hamen, help me change Alexander."

Depending on the occasion, I walk on either my hind legs or on all fours. I always go down on all fours when I need speed. I make a quick getaway by scurrying past Elena, jumping over the safety gate at the top of the stairs, and racing down to my hiding place, the cupboard under the staircase.

Once inside I begin to relax. It's happened—rarely, thank the gods—that I wasn't fast enough and Elena cornered me and made me help her change the little Pharaoh's diaper. I nearly fainted from the smell. I love the little Pharaoh, but there are some things a cat shouldn't be asked to do. It's bad enough I have to clean my own litter box!

One could ask, as I often have, why doesn't the father help? But Elena says we shouldn't disturb Gato-Hamen because he's busy. Busy! The ne'er-do-well is just reading. "He's studying," she says. "Let him be."

I'll stay in the cupboard for a while. The little Pharaoh used to fill his diapers constantly, and I've spent many hours hidden here, reminiscing.

I hear Elena's footsteps on the stairs. "Puss in Boat, where are you?" She's using my nickname to charm me out of my hiding place. No, my dear, it won't work.

"Wrappa-Hamen!"

No more sweet nicknames, eh? I hear her go back upstairs. She's given up, but I'll stay put.

It's so warm and cozy in the cupboard that I fall asleep, only to be awakened by sound of an opera playing on the record player in the library, just as *Aida* was playing both times the magic boat arrived in Elena's living room. But I don't recognize this opera.

I leave my hiding place and go into the library to find Elena and the High Priest sitting together on the couch with the little Pharaoh between them. The High Priest is snoring lightly, the book he was reading open in his hands. I join them and sit on Elena's lap, and she welcomes me with a cuddle. One of the nicest things about her is that she doesn't hold a grudge.

"What's this opera called?" I ask her.

"*Norma.*"

"What's it about?"

"Norma is a Druid high priestess. She's broken her vows by having a secret love affair with Pollione, a Roman proconsul. She's also betrayed her people. They want to go to war with the Romans, and she's kept the peace with them to protect Pollione. But now he loves a young vestal virgin."

"Poor Norma!"

"Yes. And poor Pollione. He won't give up his lover, and Norma declares war on the Romans. He breaks into the sacred cloister of the Druid virgins, is caught, and brought to Norma for judgment. A human sacrifice is needed to insure victory over the Romans, and Norma's father, the chief of the Druids, wants her to kill him with the sacrificial knife."

"So a Roman would be sacrificed to ensure victory over the Romans! Very neat."

"Yes. But it doesn't happen. Norma lies to her father. She says she wants to interrogate Pollione, but once alone with him, she promises to spare him if he will return to Rome without his lover. He refuses, and she threatens to have the woman burnt at the pyre."

"The Vizier wanted to bury me alive! Both are horrible ways to die. Norma is just as evil as the Vizier."

"No, she's not evil," Elena says. "Quite the contrary. Pollione begs her to spare his lover, and in the last scene, she tells the Druids she has a new sacrificial victim. A priestess who has betrayed her people and broken her vows. Herself!"

"Incredible."

"It's so tragic."

Elena listens more intently as the voices of Norma and Pollione become more passionate.

"A pyre is being built for her now. Norma is telling Pollione death will reunite them. He's professing his love for her and begging her to forgive him. As she's led to the pyre, he joins her to die with her . . ."

We listen as the opera comes to an end. There isn't a dry eye in the house, except for the little Pharaoh, who's too young to understand, and the High Priest, who's still fast asleep.

Elena blows her nose. "I'd better make dinner."

"Good idea. I'll help you."

"Oh, so now you want to help me, eh?"

The sarcasm isn't lost on me. I get off her lap and give her an exaggerated bow to apologize for deserting her earlier.

"Let's go," she says, laughing.

She gets up and puts the little Pharaoh on the floor. As I turn to follow her, he pulls my tail. "Wapamen, I wov u."

"I wov, I mean, I love you too, Alexander."

At night I dream of a lady dressed in bluish gray garments. She's screaming, and I can still hear her screams when I wake up. Have I been dreaming of Norma, or is this an omen?

5

Chapter 2

A few days later Elena comes home excited.

"What have you got there?" I ask, pointing to the small parcel in her hand.

"Oh, just a little something." She whispers and gestures for me to do the same.

"Is it a surprise for me?"

"No, not really."

"Elena, my feline curiosity is killing me. Please be merciful and tell me what's in the parcel!"

"Very well. But you must promise you won't tell Gato-Hamen. By the way, where is he?"

"My lips are sealed. He's in his usual spot, the library."

"I'll show you what I bought. Just let me take off my coat."

Her coat is a dark blue velvet, and she's wearing bright red gloves and matching red ankle boots. Besides being able to talk and walk like a man, I can see all the colors and shades of color humans do. I'm happy I can fully enjoy Elena's pretty outfits and her beautiful chestnut hair.

After she removes her gloves, her booties, and then her coat, she's finally ready to show me what's in the small parcel. Well, not really. "Where are my slippers?"

"The last time I saw them, they were in the library. Alexander dragged them in there."

I can tell she's debating with herself whether to look for them.

"Can't you do without them?"

"I guess I'll have to."

"Are you sure you're ready now?"

"Of course. Come into the kitchen. I'll make the two of us chocolate milk."

Another of Bastet's gifts to me, for which I'm especially grateful, is the ability to enjoy human food and drink with no ill effects.

In the kitchen, Elena puts the object of my curiosity on the table and proceeds to make chocolate milk. Seeming to move in slow motion, she takes the milk carton out of the fridge, the glasses out of a cabinet, and a spoon out of the cutlery drawer. From another cabinet she takes the bottle of liquid chocolate, lifts the cap from the top of the bottle, and squeezes the chocolate into the two glasses. After adding the milk, she stirs the contents, then takes both glasses over to the table, and at last we sit.

She takes a sip from her glass. I empty mine in a few gulps. I love chocolate milk! Then, like two conspirators, we move our chairs close together so we can talk normally instead of whispering. Elena opens the parcel and removes a small tattered old cardboard box. There's a human figure painted on top and lettering in bold capitals.

"The Rider Tarot Deck," I say aloud. Bastet also saw to it that I could read. But I can't make out the words and dates printed on the sides of the box because they're too faded. "What's inside?"

Elena opens the box and takes out a small stack of rectangular cards that look like playing cards.

"Playing cards?! This is the big secret?"

"Lower your voice, Wrappa-Hamen. These are the twenty-two major arcana Tarot cards."

"What's the difference?"

"With these, I'll be able to tell the future."

I look at her incredulously.

"Well, they say one can."

"Who are they?"

"Oh, Wrappa-Hamen, you can be exasperating sometimes. People who have been reading the Tarot cards for centuries, that's who."

I nod to make her think I understand.

"There are different versions," she says, "but all Tarot packs are based on the same principles, and all Tarot packs have seventy-eight cards. Besides the twenty-two cards called the major arcana, there are fourteen cards for each suit. They're called the lesser arcana. I bought our pack in a thrift shop. It's used and missing the lesser arcana, but I don't care. It's the major arcana cards that contain symbols and secrets from ancient cultures."

"How do you read them?"

"I don't know."

Sometimes Elena drives me to despair.

"What good are they if you don't know how to read them?" I ask her, trying to keep cool.

"I'm going to study the book."

"What book?"

"The one that explains how to read the Tarot cards, of course."

Of course. "Where's the book?" I ask, knowing it's a mistake.

"I haven't bought it yet."

"Why not?"

"The book store was out of it. I had to order it."

Now we're getting somewhere. "How long will that take?"

"A week."

This is the kind of thing the High Priest would do! I've been hoping Elena would rub off on him, not the other way around.

"Do you mean to tell me you've put me through this for nothing, that we have to wait a whole week to know the future?!"

"Shhhh, not so loud. I don't want Gato-Hamen to hear."

"Why?"

"I want to surprise him with a reading. It'll give him a kick."

The High Priest will certainly be surprised by Elena's card reading, but I'd like to give him a kick of my own—for all the times, claiming he has to study, he's neglected to help me with household chores or with changing the little Pharaoh's diapers . . .

"May I look at the cards?" I ask.

"Oh, yes, let's look."

She spreads the Tarot cards on the table. Each looks like a small painting with a title below and a number on top. The Sun is number nineteen, The Moon number eighteen, The Emperor number four—

"Elena!" It's the High Priest calling from the hall.

In a blink of an eye, she gathers the cards, makes them disappear into the little box, then gets up and hides it in one of the kitchen cabinets.

"We're in here," she says in her most innocent-sounding voice.

The High Priest comes into the kitchen and plants a kiss on her forehead.

Thank the gods I'm spared such displays of affection from him. A pat on the head is more than enough for me! I leave them to it and go upstairs to see if the little Pharaoh has woken up from his afternoon nap.

When I want time to go slow it goes fast, and when I want it to go fast it goes slow. Patience is not one of my virtues, and I dread waiting an entire week for Elena to get the book.

But the week is not uneventful. One day she goes to see if there's anything in the mailbox. The High Priest and I are alone in the library sitting on the couch when she starts to scream at the top of her lungs. We're off the couch in a flash. The book the High Priest has been reading falls on my head, and Elena's scream and mine become one.

She bursts into the library waving a magazine. "It's *Egyptian Antiquities* with my article!"

Elena is a free-lance writer and publishes many articles. She sometimes complains she gets paid very little for her work, but she says the house is paid for and the small inheritance her father left her is enough to get by on so there's no need to worry.

This article must be the one on ancient Egyptian art. The High Priest helped by giving her the benefit of his firsthand experience.

"Congratulations, my dear," he says, giving her a hug. "But why did you not tell me that it had been accepted for publication?"

"I wanted to surprise you," she says, returning the hug. "I wouldn't have been able to do it without you. Thank you, Gato-Hamen!"

"Do not be silly, Elena. My input was tiny."

The High Priest is particularly obnoxious when he pretends to be modest. I stand upright and pull on Elena's skirt to remind her that I'm here too.

"Puss in Boat, I was so excited I didn't see you," she says, bending down and kissing the top of my head.

I melt.

"Congratulations."

"Thank you, Wrappa-Hamen. I'm going to make us a special dinner to celebrate. Are you going to help me prepare it?"

I think of all the tasting I can do while helping her. "You need to ask?"

One afternoon near the end of the week, Elena comes home with the Tarot book. I thought she'd share it with me as her fellow conspirator, but, instead, she locks herself in her bedroom. Only one thing to do—lie in front of the door, and when she comes out, give her a piece of my mind.

Half an hour goes by, then another. Nothing. I'm bored. Two hours later, I fall asleep.

When I wake up, I find the bedroom door open. I look inside, but Elena and the Tarot book are nowhere to be found. I go to my bedroom to see if she's in there with the little Pharaoh. He's sleeping. But no Elena.

I hear the unmistakable noise of cutlery. She's in the kitchen. Is the High Priest there as well? I run down to the library and open the door, but only an inch. The High Priest is asleep, stretched out on the couch with a book on his lap.

The coast is clear for me to confront the traitor. I run to the kitchen, where Elena is sitting at the table about to take bite of a sandwich. Not only hasn't she shared the book with me, but she's made a snack all for herself.

"Elena!"

"You made me jump out of my skin!"

"That's only what you deserve, seeing how you've treated me."

"What are you babbling about?"

"Why didn't you share the Tarot book with me?"

"Well, I wanted to read it first by myself so, er, I could experiment on you."

"Who's babbling now? Experiment? On me? What do you mean?"

"Oh, Wrappa-Hamen, you can be so dense sometimes. I'll do my first reading for you, to get the hang of it."

An inner voice tells me to say no. But my curiosity has a louder voice. "When?" I ask before I know it.

"Now, if you like. But first let's make sure it's safe. Let's check on Gato-Hamen."

"No need. He's fast asleep. So tell me, where are the Tarot cards?"

"Right in my pocket."

"And the book?"

Elena opens the table drawer and takes it out. "Before we start, let's create an atmosphere. Close the Venetian blinds." I go to the windows and pull the cords. "That's better. Now come and sit, facing me," she orders, looking very serious.

My heart is beating fast as I watch her shuffle the cards. After a minute or so, she puts the deck in front of me. "Cut." I know what that means. In the evening the three of us sometimes play a card game. "Cut three times."

When I oblige, Elena picks up the deck, takes a card from the top, and, keeping it face down, lays it on the table while mumbling to herself. She repeats this four more times, always mumbling, till a cross is formed. Then she picks another card and places it outside the cross to the right. She's just about to turn the first card over when we hear the little Pharaoh begin to cry.

We look at each other. One of us has to see to him.

"I'll go," Elena says, getting up and placing the book on her chair. At the door, she turns around and whispers, "If you hear a whistle, it's a signal it's me coming back. But if you hear any other noise, make the cards and the book disappear."

When she leaves, I struggle with the temptation to peek at the cards. One minute goes by, then another. To pass time I give my belly a few licks, scratch behind my ears, lick between the digits of my paws, then hum.

Too impatient to wait any longer, I decide to go upstairs to see what's keeping Elena, but bump into something large and solid in the doorway.

"Did I scare you?" says the High Priest, yawning. "I came in to make myself a cup of coffee." He sees the cards on the table. "What have you been doing?"

"I, I, I . . ." Taken me by surprise, I'm at a loss for words to lie with.

"What is the matter with you? Cat got your tongue?"

Finally, I'm able to think of a fib. "I was playing solitaire."

"Oh, I love solitaire. Let me see."

I realize I've chosen the wrong fib. But there's nothing I can do about it now.

The High Priest sits in Elena's place. "Have you finished

playing?"

"Yes."

Before I can tell him not to, he picks up the Tarot deck and rifles through it. "They are unusual, these cards, different from the ones we play with. Do you mind if I take a closer look at them?"

Unusual? What an understatement. And yes, I do mind.

"Why is it so dark in here? Open the Venetian blinds."

What can I do but obey? When I go back to the table, I find the High Priest open-mouthed and looking bewildered.

"Are you all right?"

No answer. Just heavy breathing.

"I am speechless," he says finally.

Very unusual for him—it must be a sign he's terribly upset.

Unfortunately, he regains the capacity for speech within seconds. "I cannot believe this! Where in the name of Thoth have these cards come from? What sacrilege has been committed here?"

I swallow. "They're just cards."

"Just cards? They might look like just cards, but they contain ancient secret knowledge. In the Egyptian temples, figures resembling these were painted on the walls of hidden halls through which only the adepts were allowed to pass. The wall paintings were copied onto tablets and were used to read a man's future."

"Elena did say the cards have a long tradition."

"Elena? Elena is behind this?"

I've done it—I've betrayed my accomplice. I could say I've let the cat out of the bag, but the metaphor would be confusing.

"Where did Elena get these cards?" the High Priest asks angrily. Then, pointing to the ones turned face-down and arranged in the shape of a cross, he adds, "And why is she consulting them?"

"She bought them in a thrift shop because she wanted to read me my future."

"Oh, sacrilege of sacrileges!"

That's it—I've had enough. "What's the big deal I'd like to know?"

"Oh, you ignoramus of a cat, the door of destiny has been pushed open."

He closes his eyes and brings a hand to his forehead. When the

12

High Priest does that, it's serious. It's best not to interrupt him by trying to reason with him, but to let him play out his drama to the end. It might take a long time, so I might just as well sit down.

After a few minutes, he opens his eyes, puts both hands on the table, and leans forward. "There is nothing for it." He shakes his head in disbelief and sighs profusely. "Once the door is open, we must enter. We must read the cards Elena has placed here. What did she say as she placed the cards face-down in the form of a cross?"

"I don't know. She was mumbling. Would that be important?"

"Oh, ignoramus cat, in our ancient time, when a priest consulted the tablets to read a man's future—and this was allowed only in special circumstances—the position of each tablet had a meaning and the arrangement determined the sequence in which the cards were read."

"I'm beginning to understand."

"Finally! And now we must wait for your accomplice before I can make heads or tail out of this arrangement."

"We don't need to wait for my accomplice, I mean, Elena. You can use the book."

"Book? You mean she was following instructions in a book?"

"Yes, and you're sitting on it."

He puts a hand under himself, then, cursing, produces the book and begins to flip through it.

"Here it is, under 'card spread,'" he says after a minute. He reads, taking his time, and nods, as if agreeing. "Now that I understand the meaning of this arrangement, I can read the cards properly." He closes the book and brings his fist down on it. "Let us get to work."

He points to the card forming the bottom of the cross. "This card stands for your past and its influence on your present."

He turns it over. It's numbered zero and called the Fool. It's a picture of a young man with a small dog at his heels. Unwittingly, for his nose is in the air, he's about to step over a precipice.

"You mean I was a fool in the past? Does the zero mean I'm a failure?"

The High Priest sighs heavily. "Ignoramus cat, the image should not be interpreted simplistically, and an obvious

13

interpretation is seldom the right one. A reading is primarily the result of the diviner's intuition. He must become one with each tablet . . . and I cannot do that if you keep interrupting. So be a good cat and promise to be quiet."

"I'm sorry," I say, then add reluctantly, "I promise to be quiet."

He clears his throat, then speaks in a loud voice, stressing every syllable. "Wrappa-Hamen, you are unique—a cat who has been given the ability to speak and walk like a man. You are about to embark on a journey, and who you are will determine where you go."

I remain silent.

The High Priest turns over the card forming the left arm of the cross. It's number nine, the Hermit—a bearded old man wearing a cloak and carrying a staff in one hand and a lantern in the other.

"This card stands for the obstacles you will encounter. Time, time will be against you."

Again, I remain silent.

Next, he turns over the card forming the right arm of the cross. Number eight, Strength. There's a picture of a woman holding the mouth of a lion closed with her bare hands.

"This card stands for the influences in your favor. You have a strong character. That quality will see you through the demands to be made of you." Then, closing his eyes, he recites,

> I am One that transforms into Two.
> I am Two that transforms into Four.
> I am Four that transforms into Eight.
> After this I am One.

As much as I would like to ask questions, I keep my promise and remain quiet.

The High Priest opens his eyes and looks at me intensely. "Your old self you will shed to become him again and yet new."

He turns over the card forming the top of the cross. Number two, the High Priestess. It shows a woman dressed in veils, sitting on a throne set between two pillars and holding a book in her left hand.

"In the near future, you will meet a high priestess."

This time, I can't stop myself. "You've just told me the obvious interpretation is never the right one."

"No, I did not. I said it was seldom the right one. Now, be quiet and do not interrupt again. You will meet a high priestess, and she will reveal secrets to you."

When he gives no further explanation, I ask, "What secrets?"

"I have no idea . . . Did I not tell you to be quiet?" he says as he turns over the middle card.

It's number six, the Lovers. An angel with outspread wings hovers over a naked man and woman.

The High Priest sighs, grunts, and shakes his head. But how can such a lovely image represent something bad? Maybe he's upset because it's upside down, so I put it right side up.

"Ignoramus cat," he yells. "What in the name of the gods do you think you are doing? An inverted card is read differently than if it were right side up."

If he calls me "ignoramus cat" one more time . . .

He returns the card to its original position. I try to look contrite and wait for him to interpret the card—impatiently, I may add.

"Ah, the secrets you learn from the high priestess will, in your distant future, bring you face to face with an evil force," he says, slamming his fists on the table. "A choice, Wrappa-Hamen, a painful choice will be asked of you."

Why did I let Elena convince me to have a Tarot reading? Why didn't I listen to the inner voice that told me to be wary? You know why, I say to myself. It's because you're a damn curious beast.

As if my thoughts have summoned her, Elena makes her entrance, holding the little Pharaoh in her arms. "I heard everything. I was outside listening, but didn't have the courage to come in."

She joins us at the table, the little Pharaoh in her lap.

"Oh, Elena, Elena, why?" the High Priest says, looking across at her and shaking his head. "But we must continue. Let us look at the final card." It's the one placed outside the cross.

"It stands for the final outcome and its effect on Wrappa-

Hamen," she says proudly.

A dirty look from the High Priest warns her not to say anything more. Just as he reaches to turn the card, the little Pharaoh leans forward from Elena's lap, grabs the card, and returns it to the deck, knocking the deck onto the floor in the process.

The cross is still there but the crucial card is gone. The little Pharaoh looks down at the mess he's made, turns to me, and smiles.

The High Priest kneels on the floor to gather the cards, and, when he gets up, adds the five cards lying on the table and neatens the deck into a tight pack, which he clutches angrily. "I am confiscating these and the book!"

As he leaves the kitchen, he turns around to give us a look of utter contempt.

When he's gone, Elena starts on me. "Well, you gave me up right away."

"Do you think I should have told him I fabricated the cards and the book out of thin air?"

My sarcasm is lost on her. "You could have tried."

"I don't see what you're so upset about. I'm the one who will come to face to face with an evil force—"

"Before I brought home the Tarot cards and the book, you didn't know any part of your future."

"That's exactly my point. I was ignorant and happy."

No reply? Usually Elena wants to have the last word.

She's thinking. Here it comes. "Ingrate."

In a huff, she pulls the little Pharaoh to her chest, gets up from the table, and turns her back to me. As she walks out of the kitchen, the Pharaoh sticks his head up over her shoulder and waves good bye. I wave back.

While reflecting on all that's happened, I make myself my favorite sandwich. Baloney on white bread with mustard. "Thank you, Bastet!" I say as I take a bite.

Chapter 3

No one says a word about the Tarot reading in the days that follow. I seem to be the only one concerned about my future. The High Priest has closed the book, so to speak, on the incident. Elena has moved on to another interest, painting with watercolors.

The house is filling up with portraits of me. Maybe the artist in Elena is drawn to my shiny silver coat, lapis-blue eyes, and full-figured feline form. Or am I the only model she has because the High Priest is too impatient and the Pharaoh moves continuously? Not that I've much else to do, but I'm bored with posing hour after hour.

One day a reprieve comes in the form of a letter. Elena and I are in the den—I've just taken my pose, and she's just sat down and lifted her brush in the air—when our cozy little world is disrupted by the loud ring of the doorbell. Quickly getting up to answer the door, Elena bumps into the small table by her side. The two chalice-shaped glasses filled with water which she keeps on top—one to wet her brushes, the other to clean them—topple over.

"Darn it!" she says, dropping her brush and straightening the half empty glasses. Then she shouts, "Gato-Hamen! Answer the door!"

It's about time the ne'er-do-well is asked to do something.

Elena is wiping the water from the table with some tissues when the High Priest enters the den and presents her with an envelope. "Express mail from England," he says.

Elena dries her hands on her artist's apron and takes the envelope from him. She studies it before opening it, as if trying to tell what's inside.

Open it already!

She slides the handle of a paint brush under the flap of the envelope, tears it open, then takes a letter out and reads it silently. She becomes so excited her hand trembles as she puts the letter down.

"What does it say?!" the High Priest and I ask in unison.

"It's from a lady who lives in Bath," Elena replies. "She's interested in Egyptology and has read my article in *Egyptian Antiquities*. She's so impressed by my writing and expertise that she'd like me to write her biography. She spent much of her childhood in Egypt and has many interesting anecdotes to relate."

"Very flattering," the High Priest says. "And it sounds like an interesting project."

"There's more! She's offering me an advance of 5,000 pounds against 50% of all royalties, and she wants me to stay in her home in Bath while I write her biography. She says if I have a family they're invited as well, all expenses paid. What do you think, Gato-Hamen? Do you think I should accept the offer?"

"Of course."

"It's so tempting, especially since some of my best memories are of that beautiful city. I spent an entire summer in Bath when I was a child. My mother and I stayed there while my father was in London working on an archaeological project for the British Museum. He would come and visit on the weekends."

"Even more reason to accept."

"But I won't go without my family!"

"I would love to accompany you, Elena."

"Is anybody going to ask me?" I say.

"I didn't ask you, Puss in Boat, because I know you'd want to go if only out of curiosity."

She reads me like a book.

"But how can we all travel to England? You, Gato-Hamen, have no documents. As far as the world is concerned, you don't exist." The non-existence of the High Priest is an appealing concept!

I try to interrupt her. "I'd like to say something."

But she ignores me and continues. "There's nothing to discuss. I've made my decision. If we can't all go, I won't go."

I can't stand this nonsense any longer. "Am I the only one who's thinking in this crazy household? Obviously you've forgotten we have the magic boat."

Elena and the High Priest look at me in awe.

"My hero!" she says. "I'd forgotten about the boat."

"I as well," he admits.

I do wonder about these two. How could they have forgotten about the boat? It's been standing in the middle of the library since our return from Egypt. Elena covered it with white sheets to protect it from dust. It looks like a large mummy.

"Do you think it can take us to England?" she asks, looking at the High Priest.

"I do not know. We can try. But I would never put you and Alexander in danger. I want you two to go by plane. Wrappa-Hamen and I will go on the boat."

Why is it all right for me to be in danger? But if it means not having to spend countless hours posing for Elena, I'm willing to take the risk. Anyway, I'm ready for some adventure.

"I hate to admit it, but you're right," she says. "Alexander and I will fly."

"But there is another problem which needs to be addressed," the High Priest says.

"What?"

"The boat cannot appear in the middle of Bath. Do you remember the city well enough to tell us of a safe place?"

"Yes and no."

"Which is it?" the High Priest and I ask in unison.

"What I'm trying to say is, it's been almost thirty years, and I'm not sure I can rely on my childhood memories."

"Then you will need to arrive in Bath first," the High Priest says. "You can reconnoiter a bit and then let us know where we can appear safely."

"You're right, Gato-Hamen. I should go first and find a safe place for the boat to materialize."

"So it is settled?"

"Yes!"

Finally, I say to myself.

It's only hours later that the nickel drops. The Tarot card reading predicted a journey. Coincidence? I hope so. I don't relish the thought of coming face to face with an evil force!

But when I ask the High Priest for some reassurance on the matter, his comments are the opposite of reassuring.

"There is no such thing as coincidence. What the cards have foretold has begun to unfold."

Chapter 4

Elena has written back to the lady in Bath accepting her offer. She's also decided that she and the High Priest need new clothing. They go out shopping everyday, and in the evening I'm treated to a fashion show. I enjoy looking at Elena walking up and down the hallway wearing her new outfits, but I could live without the High Priest doing the same in his.

Instead of clothing, I get a pet carrier bag. It has a shoulder strap for the High Priest, the bottom is nicely padded for comfort, and all four sides are made of fine mesh, giving me an unobstructed view. I test it by having my own fashion show. The High Priest carries me up and down the hallway while Elena watches.

But there's no time to test my carrier bag outdoors. Elena says she has all sorts of things to do which, according to her, are more important. As if watering the plants is more important! Sometimes I feel I'm taken for granted.

The refrigerator door is soon covered with her notes. Most of them are instructions for the High Priest. "Don't forget to give the keys to the next-door neighbor before you leave, so he can water the plants." "Don't forget to ask the mailman to hold the mail."

But some of the notes are instructions for me. One reads, "Don't forget to clean your litter box everyday."

How insulting! It's almost enough to make me regret I can read.

On the day of Elena's departure I'm in my bedroom playing with the little Pharaoh for the last time until we're all together again in England.

"Where is my passport?" she yells from her bedroom. "I can't find my passport!"

As I'm learning, traveling is very stressful for humans.

"You put it in your purse five minutes ago," the High Priest tells her.

I hear the exasperation in his voice. Unfortunately, I also hear all the sweet nothings she's telling him as a way of thanking him for his patience.

After Elena looks in her purse to reassure herself her passport is there, she tells the High Priest to take her suitcases downstairs, stand in the front of the building, and hail a taxi. A few moments later, he's in the foyer, shouting up at us to come down because the taxi is waiting.

I follow Elena as she heads downstairs and out into the street with the Pharaoh in her arms. After a kiss here and a kiss there, a hug here and a hug there, and after she has the High Priest swear he's put all her luggage in the trunk of the taxi and she's given us her final instructions, she and the Pharaoh are waving goodbye from the back seat. The High Priest waves back.

I can't because I'm acting like a normal cat—if such a thing exists.

In a few seconds Elena and the Pharaoh are out of sight, gone. The High Priest and I try to go back inside—only to discover the front door has closed behind us and locked automatically, and he's forgotten his keys.

So much for Elena's warnings.

"Gato-Hamen, you're hopeless!"

"It was the excitement," he says meekly.

"We can't get in through the back door either. Elena always keeps it locked. Let's see if we can find an open window."

"Good idea."

None of the front windows are open, so we go down the small alley separating Elena's house from the building next to it and enter the backyard. None of the back windows are open on the first floor, but on the second floor her parents' bedroom window is open a few inches.

Elena hardly goes in there. Too many memories, she says.

The High Priest points to the open window. "Do you think you can climb up there?"

"I haven't climbed up anything in a long time, but I'll give it a try."

What's the best way to reach the window? The trellis running up the wall might act as a ladder. I test it, first with my forepaws, then with my hindpaws. It seems strong enough to hold my weight, and I begin to climb, monitored by a very anxious High Priest.

"Please be careful. If you get hurt, Elena will never forgive me."

Elena will never forgive him? I'll never forgive him! I wouldn't be risking my life if he hadn't been so absent-minded as to lock us out.

"Be careful!"

The High Priest has broken my concentration, and my left hindpaw misses a step. I curse him under my breath.

I continue to climb with no further warnings from below and no further missteps until I'm level with the open window. It's about a foot away on my right. I stretch my forepaw toward the windowsill. I've barely touched it when I lose my balance and find myself hanging by the claws of one paw.

"For the love of Thoth!" says the High Priest.

Doing my best to ignore his panic, I manage to dig the claws of my other forepaw into the windowsill and, with all the strength both paws can muster, pull myself up. There's very little room on the windowsill. Carefully, I push my head through the small opening between it and the bottom of the window—

I can't believe this! I'm stuck! My head is half in, half out.

Unfortunately my ears are out, and I hear the High Priest shout, "What is taking so long?"

He won't be able to hear them anyway, so I stifle the curses that come to mind. I'll use them when he's right in front of me. But when will that be? I don't seem to be able to move forwards or backwards.

"Well?" I hear from below.

That does it! I must get unstuck so I can kick him in the shins. I try to push the window up with my head, but it's too heavy, and all I get for my efforts is a sudden headache. Next I try to force my entire head through the opening, but I scrape the top of it on the rough wood.

"Wrappa-Hamen, do not keep messing about! Just go inside!"

His words make me angrier, but also stronger. When I try to push the window up this time, it moves slightly, and the opening is now wide enough for me to wiggle through.

Once inside, I shut the window so I can no longer hear the High Priest. It's chilly in here. The furniture is covered in dusty white sheets—

For the love of the gods! There's a cat on his hind paws in the middle of the room! My fur stands up, I hiss, and the cat hisses back—

It's a good thing no one's here to see this. I'm hissing at my own image in a table mirror. What would the High Priest have to say?

I've almost forgotten about him. I go back to the window and look down. He's gesticulating, but he can wait. I haven't been in this bedroom since he performed the Entering to retrieve from Elena's memory the ancient Egyptian spell to revive the dead. I had to use all my ingenuity—and my tail—to pull him out of the room, or he would have remained trapped in her memory . . .

Ah, the High Priest. I look out the window again. He's still gesticulating. I should stop reminiscing and go downstairs to open the back door for him.

As I turn from the window, I again see an image in the mirror. I tell myself I'm not going to be fooled twice, but what I see in the mirror isn't my reflection. It's a tall woman with her arms stretched toward me. I turn and look behind me, but there isn't anyone there.

It's probably the curtains moving in the wind. But I closed the window when I came in.

I look into the mirror again. The woman is still there. I've seen her before. It was the woman in my dream who made me think of Norma.

She begins to wail. The sound congeals my blood. She brings her hands to her face as if in absolute despair, and her wails grow louder. Never in my life have I heard such mournful cries!

Though terrified, I have an uncontrollable urge to comfort her. I must touch her. I extend my paw. But in a blink of an eye she's gone, leaving only the echoes of her cries.

Then I hear another sort of crying. No, it's cursing, and it's coming from the garden. I'd better get downstairs and open the back door for the High Priest.

As a very angry man enters the house, the telephone rings. "It must be Elena," he says. "She told me she would call us from the airport."

He runs like a madman to the phone in the hallway, and I follow him like a mad cat. If that phone stops ringing, we're doomed. She'll come back from the airport.

Actually, it's only the High Priest who should be worried. After all, he's the one who locked us out. If Elena knew, he'd think hell more pleasant than facing her. I could almost feel sorry for him. Almost!

He reaches the phone before it stops ringing. "Oh yes, my dear," he says, breathless. "I was just in the kitchen making our supper."

I jump on top of the small table where the phone sits. I hear Elena loud and clear. "Why didn't you answer the phone in the kitchen?"

A good question.

"I do not know. I forgot there was one."

A poor answer. But she seems to accept it. "Let me talk to Wrappa-Hamen."

Holding the large old-fashioned receiver in both forepaws, I put it to my ear. "Please take care of Gato-Hamen. You know how absentminded he can be."

An understatement!

"Don't worry about him. Please give Alexander a big lick for me."

"Well, I'll give him a big kiss. Good bye then. I'll call from England."

"Good bye, Elena."

When I hang up, the High Priest is staring at me with a look of horror.

"What in the name of the gods is wrong with you?" I ask him. "Why are you looking at me like that?"

"You are bleeding from a gash in the top of your head!"

I touch my head, and when I look at my paw, it's covered in blood. My hindlegs give out from under me. The last thing I see is the High Priest moving to catch me . . .

When I regain consciousness, I'm lying on the kitchen table. He's looming large over me, and in his hand is a threaded needle.

"What are you doing?"

"I am going to stitch the gash on your head." That's the last thing I hear before I faint again.

When I wake up, I'm in my bed. The top of my head is sore, and when I touch it, I feel a bandage. Where's the butcher?

"Gato-Hamen!"

I hear him hurrying up the stairs. He enters the room carrying a bowl, pulls a chair over to the bed, sits down, and switches on the bedside lamp. The sudden light hurts my eyes.

"I have brought you a bowl of milk," he says.

"Never mind that. What have you done to me?"

"I have sewn up the gash in your head. Do not worry. It took only five stitches."

"My star, my star!"

When the Pharaoh was resurrected after I told Bastet I was willing to give my life for his, he took me up in his arms and kissed me on the brow, burning a white star upon it.

"Your star is fine," says the High Priest. "The wound is to the side of it."

"Wait until Elena finds out!"

"Please, please, Wrappa-Hamen, do not tell her about your injury."

"Don't you think she'll ask when she sees it?"

"She will not see it. You will be wearing a bandage."

"Won't she ask why my head is bandaged?"

The nickel drops. "Please," he begs, "do not tell her it was my fault. I will do anything you want."

Have I heard him correctly? "Did you just say you'd do anything I want?"

"Yes, yes. What is it you wish?"

"I don't know yet. I'll let you know."

I have to give this serious thought. It's not every day such an opportunity arises.

"Let me rest now. Turn off the light," I say in a whisper.

The High Priest turns the light off and gets up to leave. Just to keep him on his toes, I give him a long pained "Meeeeeoooooow" as a send-off. Maybe it's the darkness, or maybe my meow has touched a nerve, but he bangs his knee hard on the Pharaoh's toy chest.

Only five stitches? Well, only a bump on the knee.

When I'm alone, I run my paw over the star the Pharaoh

25

burned on my brow with his kiss, the indelible symbol of our friendship. Then I succumb to sleep.

Chapter 5

I wake up in the morning confused. I put a paw to my head. The bandage is still there, but I can't really say my head hurts. I have only a vague recollection of the woman in the mirror. She must've been the result of my head injury.

What's that gurgling sound?

It's my stomach complaining. And no wonder—I had no supper last night!

I give myself a thorough lick, ease myself out of bed, and head for the kitchen, where the High Priest is making pancakes. I take my place at the table. "Good morning. That smells good."

"Good morning, Wrappa-Hamen. How do you feel? How is your head?"

He turns the gas off and, with his spatula, scoops up the last pancake from the grill and carries it over to the table. The spatula hovers over his plate. There are already more pancakes on it than on mine. My head feels fine, but it won't hurt to complain a bit. Guilt is a powerful tool.

"I've a headache," I say in a sad voice.

It works. The High Priest moves the spatula over to my plate, drops the pancake on it, then sits at the table.

"Will you pass me the maple syrup?" I ask. I love maple syrup. Ancient Egypt had honey, but this is even more delicious! I pour the amber liquid on top of my pancakes and begin to eat.

"You might have a headache. But your appetite is not impaired."

I ignore the High Priest's sarcastic remark and take another forkful of the pancakes.

"Elena will not call until this evening," he says. "What would you say to an outing?"

"Didn't she give us specific orders not to go out?"

Not that I don't like the idea of going out. It's just that if Elena ever discovers we disobeyed her, she'll never forgive us—especially me, since she told me to take care of the High Priest.

"We can stay in the area," he insists. "Trust me. We will be all right."

I'm a cat after all, and curiosity wins over caution.

"Let's do it."

"That is the spirit."

Anxious to be get started, we finish breakfast in a hurry.

The High Priest puts me in the pet carrier bag with the mesh sides and slings the strap over his shoulder. I find myself at his hip.

"Have you got the house keys?" I ask him just before he shuts the door.

He dangles them in front of my nose, meaning, "What do you take me for?"

I take him for the same forgetful man who locked us out only yesterday!

At the sound of the keys turning in the locks, I remember we're disobeying Elena and feel a pang of guilt. But it's not strong enough to make me want to abandon our adventure.

"Here we go," the High Priest says enthusiastically.

"Do you have a plan?'

"I would like to buy Elena a gift."

"But then she'll know we went out."

"I will tell her I conjured it up, using an ancient magical spell."

It'll be magic if he manages to convince her of that!

"What did you have in mind?"

"A plant."

"She won't see it for a long time. Or are you planning to take it with us on the boat when we leave?"

"No. No such thing. It will be here when she comes back."

The High Priest seems so happy I don't have the heart to tell him his choice of gift stinks.

When we get to Broadway, he stops. "Let me get my bearings. As I remember, around here there is a shop that sells plants . . . Oh yes, there it is, on the other side."

The light is green, and we cross the street. The door of the shop is open. We go in and stop in front of a counter with a sullen-looking woman standing behind it. She's talking—barking is more accurate—to a young man. "And don't you take three hours to bring back a cup of coffee!" Her eyes follow the young man till he's left.

The High Priest moves closer to the counter, so close that the front of the carrier bag is pushed up against it and I can no longer see the woman. Which is just as well.

"Can I help?" she says, still barking.

"I would like to buy my wife a plant."

"Do you know what ki—?" A sneeze prevents the woman from finishing her question.

"Something pretty," the High Priest says. "Something with flowers."

"What about pink geraniums?" She sneezes again.

"Never heard of them."

The woman is probably asking herself what planet this guy has been living on—I know how she feels.

I hear her sigh, walk to the back of the store, then return. "Here it is," she announces. "A geranium plant."

There's a thud as something is placed on the counter. It must be a flowerpot.

"But there are no flowers," the High Priest says.

"There will be in a few weeks."

He isn't convinced. "Can I see something else?"

The woman sighs again. Then, I hear a series of loud sneezes. Out of reflex, I retreat to the back of the carrier bag.

"What are you carrying?" she asks the High Priest. She must have finally noticed the shoulder strap.

He lifts the carrier bag and places it on the counter beside the flowerpot.

"Is that a cat in there?"

The answer should be obvious.

"I hate cats. They give me allergies." The woman sneezes again. "And what's that on its head? A bandage? It's not diseased, is it?"

"No, no. It is, I mean, he, is fine,"

I rub fur from my chest and blow it toward the woman. More sneezes, then tears begin to stream down her face.

"May I see another plant?" the High Priest asks.

The woman wipes her nose with a dirty handkerchief, then walks away again and comes back with another plant. "This is a cactus."

It looks like a small tower made of green eggs dotted with thorns and tiny flowers.

"Your wife will love it. It practically takes care of itself." She gives me a dirty look and rubs her eyes.

"That is wonderful," the High Priest says. "I will take it."

There's no accounting for taste.

The woman seems relieved. She wraps the plant in plastic and hands it to him. "How will you be paying?" I count three more sneezes.

The High Priest reaches into his pocket, but his hand comes out empty. I remembered to ask him if he had the keys, but not if he had money. No wonder Elena doesn't want us to go out alone. In the year we've been with her she's grown to know him well.

"May I take the plant and come back with the money? I will leave the cat here as security."

Leave me with that sneezing monster? I curse him under my breath.

The woman's curses are even worse. "I don't want your diseased cat!" she says. "Take the cactus and stuff it."

Stuff it with what? Humans say the funniest things.

The High Priest takes the carrier bag and the cactus from the counter.

"I can't believe it!" the woman screams as he walks towards the door. "He's actually taking it!"

Whom is she talking to? We're the only ones here. Is that a bag of dirt that flew past us?

The High Priest walks faster. He pushes the door open, and now that we're outside, I can talk. "I want to go home!"

"Wrappa-Hamen, where is your sense of adventure, your . . . ?"

"Gone."

"It was a minor setback. We have faced much worse, you and I."

True, but old sneezy was pretty scary.

The High Priest puts the carrier bag down, unzips the top, and places his hand inside to give me a reassuring pat on my bandaged head.

I relent. "All right. Let's go on."

He zips the carrier bag, lifts it back to his hip, and we continue down Broadway.

Chapter 6

People are spilling out of the mouth of hell—that's what Elena calls the entrance to the subway. She refuses to take it, and I don't blame her. I've seen subways on television, and that's close enough for me.

All the unhappy travelers seem upset, and some are cursing. Most of them join the crowd walking down Broadway, while others get on the line at the bus stop. The very desperate are hailing a taxi.

It's a warm, sunny day, and I'm happy to be outdoors. I'd be happier if it weren't for some of the smells. The smell from the rear of a car is quite offensive, and the smell from the rear of a bus is even worse. It's like an elephant fart.

But there are smells I like, such as the smell of cooking food coming from restaurants. I enjoy trying to guess what's being cooked—it's tomato sauce in the Italian restaurant we're passing now. I also like the smell of perfume, and the shapely girl sashaying by leaves in her wake a fragrance that reminds me of the perfume I used to smell at court in ancient Egypt.

"Let us leave all this hustle and bustle behind," says the High Priest, turning off Broadway.

We go down a large wide street lined with trees. Birds perched on branches are practicing their spring songs. The street is deserted except for a few passersby and an occasional car driving slowly, probably looking for a parking space.

In the distance I see three women sitting in big chairs arranged in a row. As we approach them, I realize they're old women and their chairs have wheels, like chariots. Two of them are sleeping with their mouths open.

They remind me of Egyptian mummies.

The woman in the middle is very much awake and is looking at us with suspicion, her gaze going back and forth from the High Priest to me. She reaches into the pocket of her sweater, takes out a pair of eyeglasses, and puts them on.

"Good morning," the High Priest says.

"You're late!" she yells back.

"I beg your pardon? You must be mistaking me for someone

32

else."

"I'm not mistaken. You were supposed to come yesterday with a dog. Instead, you show up today with a cat."

The High Priest, for once, is at a loss for words.

In the meantime one of the mummies, I mean, one of the other old women, wakes up. She looks disoriented.

I know how she feels. I'm always disoriented when I wake up from a nap.

She studies the High Priest, then turns toward the other woman. "Rosa, who's this man?"

"He's the man from the Animal Society."

"The man from the Animal Society," she says, carefully pronouncing every syllable.

"I just said that, Pauline," Rosa barks back at her. "Do you always have to repeat what I say?"

"I'm sorry," Pauline says meekly. Then, as if her life depended on waking up the old woman still sleeping, she yells, "Nanette, wake up, wake up! Look who's here!"

"Who's here?!" Nanette says, jumping up in her chair. "Why do you always say 'look.' You know I can't see. So who the hell is here, eh?"

"He's the man from the Animal Society," Pauline says before the High Priest can speak.

"Rosa, the man from the Animal Society is here," Nanette says, excited.

"For crying out loud, I know," yells Rosa, exasperated. Then, looking at the High Priest, she orders, "Take the cat out of the bag."

If he had any brains, he'd flee. Instead—and I'm not surprised by this—he nods at Rosa, puts the cactus and my carrier bag on the ground, squats, and unzips the case. He puts his hands in, and I give one a bite. He quickly withdraws them and sucks on the injured one.

"He's a feisty one, isn't he?" Rosa observes.

"He's got chutzpah," Pauline says.

The High Priest mumbles something abusive in my direction, then leans close to me to whisper in my ear. "Be good, Wrappa-Hamen. They are just harmless old women."

I'd like to tell him Rosa doesn't look at all harmless. She's a stocky woman with a glint of mischief in her eyes.

Cautiously, the High Priest lifts me out of the carrier bag and sets me on the pavement.

"Oh," cries Pauline. "What a fat cat!"

"Mamma mia!" Rosa exclaims, clapping her hands. "What's the matter with his head?"

"He had a minor accident. Nothing to worry about."

Minor accident, my rump! Nothing to worry about, eh? That's not what Elena would say.

"When I was a kid," Pauline says, "I wanted a cat, but my parents wouldn't allow it. They said cats were unclean."

Unclean? But we're always licking ourselves!

"What's his name?" asks Nanette, the blind one.

"His name is Wrappa-Hamen."

"What kind of name is that?" asks Rosa. "Gastone. Now, that's a cat's name." She looks at me and says, "Right, Gastone?"

Not very Egyptian. But I guess I have to put up with it till we get away from here.

"That is also a nice name," says the High Priest, sounding conciliatory.

"Put Gastone here," Rosa orders, pointing at her lap.

He obeys, and as soon as I'm on her lap, her hands encircle my midriff. As I suspected, she has strong hands. She puts her face close to mine. Her eyeglasses tickle my nose.

"Before the war, cats in Rome strutted about as if they owned the place. People used to feed them. During the war, you couldn't find one."

Cats are smart. They obviously left the city in search of a more peaceful place.

"People were starving. All the cats were eaten."

I swallow hard.

"Gastone would have fed a family of five!"

I swallow again, almost choking.

I'm about to bite Rosa when she takes one hand from my midriff and begins to stroke me. She's obviously done this with other cats because she knows exactly where the trigger points are. Despite myself, I begin to purr.

She resumes talking, but instead of yelling as she's been doing, she talks in a normal tone.

"I had a cat named Gastone. It was March 23, 1943, and I had gone to Via Arcione to pick him up from the veterinarian. With Gastone in a cardboard box, I had just left the vet, who had his practice on the ground floor, and was walking through the courtyard when I heard an explosion. I ran through the portone and saw people running desperately down the street. 'Run, run!' someone yelled at me. 'Germans soldiers were killed. The Germans will want revenge. Run!'"

Rosa stops for a moment, as if she's been running and has to catch her breath.

The High Priest asks what I want to, but can't. "What happened then?"

"I stood in front of the portone petrified, not knowing if it was safer to go back in or to run away from the neighborhood as fast as my legs could carry me. Then someone bumped into me, knocking the cardboard box to the ground. It opened and Gastone ran off. I wanted to run after him, but a young man grabbed me by the arm and dragged me away. I yelled at him to let me go. I cursed at him, but it was no use. The young man was intent on saving my life."

Rosa stops talking again, her face streaked with tears. When she continues her story, it seems to require a great effort.

"As soon as I got home I went to the window to watch for Gastone, in case by some miracle he might find his way home. My mother couldn't drag me from the window. I stayed there all evening and all night. But Gastone never came home—and three hundred thirty-five men were never to see their families again. They were killed by the Germans in reprisal for the bombing . . . I haven't spoken of this before. There's something about this cat that made me want to tell it now."

The silence that's fallen is broken by Pauline. "Did that young man Gastone ever come back?"

"It was the veterinarian who was named Gastone," says Nanette, shaking her head at Pauline.

"Go to sleep, you two!" Rosa says, having gone back to yelling. "You drive me crazy."

"Stop yelling," Pauline complains. "I'm not deaf!"

35

Nanette obeys Rosa and closes her eyes, but Pauline reaches over to Rosa's lap and puts her hand on my back. At first her touch is hesitant. Then she begins to pet me.

I look up at the High Priest. He's smiling.

It's become overcast, and drops of rain begin to fall. "It's time to go," he says, lifting me gently from Rosa's lap.

He puts me back in the carrier bag, lifts it from the pavement, and puts the strap over his shoulder. He's about to zipper it when the doors to the building we're in front of swing open. For the first time, I notice the sign over the door. Home for the Aged.

Three plump women come out dressed in white—they even wear white shoes. They walk towards us, and when they reach the old women they separate, each going behind a chair.

"All right, ladies. Time to go in," the one behind Rosa's chair announces cheerfully.

The High Priest stands aside, and the women in white start to push the chairs.

"Are you going to tell me who that man was?" asks the woman pushing Pauline's chair. "Or are you keeping it a secret?"

"He's the man from the Animal Society."

"Oh, Pauline, you know very well the Animal Society sends a lady and she only comes once a week. She came yesterday with a puppy. Remember?"

"I do," says Pauline, sounding hurt. "But Rosa told me that man was from the Animal Society."

Rosa doesn't deny it. She'd rather let her friends think she made a mistake than admit she wanted a chance to hold me on her lap and pet me.

When she saw me, she saw her Gastone. I guess he was also gray and had a patch of white on his head, a patch resembling my bandage.

When the chairs get close to the doors, they open again, as if by magic. The High Priest stands by the entrance so he can say goodbye to each woman as she's pushed inside. First Rosa, then Pauline. As Nanette is being pushed past us, the woman in white stops and reaches inside the carrier bag to pet me. "Oh, my. Whoever bandaged the cat did a good job."

Good job indeed!

36

Nanette beckons to the High Priest—she wants to pet me as well.

The High Priest bends over her and places the carrier bag directly in front of her. I stand on my hind legs, lean out of the carrier bag, and put my paws on Nanette's shoulder. She places her hand on my back, but doesn't stroke me. Her frail, bony hand just rests there.

"He's the one!" she cries out. "He's the one!"

"It's all right, Nanette. It's all right," the woman in white says, like a parent talking to a frightened child.

Nanette's hand falls from my back as she's pushed inside. Then the door shuts, sealing the three old women in, as if in a tomb.

The High Priest and I look at each other.

"What do you think that was all about?" I ask. "She scared me."

"I am sure she did not mean to scare you. It is a very lonely place in there, and, being blind, she must feel even lonelier than the others. It is only natural she became excited by contact with strangers."

He's right. I feel compassion for all three old women, but especially Nanette.

We resume walking down the street when I remember the High Priest said he would grant me a wish.

"About that wish you . . ."

"Yes?"

"I thought about it. I know what I want."

"And what is that, Gastone, I mean, Wrappa-Hamen?"

"I want us to come back here sometime."

"Granted."

I decide to forgive him for the stitches on my head.

Chapter 7

Only when we get back home does the High Priest realize he's left the cactus behind on the sidewalk in front of the home where the old women live.

"Now I have no present for Elena."

"You can get her something when we get to England." What I don't say is that I doubt very much Elena would have wanted a plant looking like green eggs with thorns.

And speak of the devil. The phone rings and the High Priest answers. "It's Elena."

I jump up onto the little table where the phone is kept and get up on my hind legs so I can put my ear close to the receiver.

"You are calling earlier than you said you would," the High Priest says.

"I'm very tired from the trip and would like to go to sleep."

"How is Alexander?"

"He's just fine. He slept for almost the entire flight and on the train ride from London to Bath."

"Have you met your hostess?"

"No. She won't be back for a few days. She sent her majordomo to pick me up at the train station, and he's looking after me."

"How is the house?"

"It's gorgeous. It's in the Royal Crescent. The view from the front windows is spectacular. There's a luxury hotel a few doors away, and I've been given a card so I can use the hotel spa. I was there earlier to swim in the pool, which is modeled on a Roman bath . . . But tell me about you."

"Not much to say. Wrappa-Hamen spent the day listening to music, and I was reading."

I hope Elena can't tell the High Priest is lying.

"Well, goodnight, my dear," she says, yawning. "We'll talk tomorrow about your coming here." She adds, "I love you."

"I love you too."

"What am I, chopped liver?" I say.

"I love you too, Puss in Boat."

That's better! I hear a click. She's hung up.

"What's for dinner?" I ask the High Priest.

"A surprise."

"Something I've had before?"

"Maybe," he says, nudging me out of the kitchen.

Off I go to the library. Should I listen to an opera, browse through a magazine, or take a nap?

I choose the nap, but then see the electric train set.

A few days before Elena received the letter from England she found the dusty boxes in the attic and brought them down to the kitchen. The electric train belonged to her father, she said, but both of them used to play with it, and she thought the three of us would have fun setting it up and playing with it together.

But first the entire train set had to be cleaned.

Elena polished the steam locomotive and the passenger cars. The High Priest was given the task of shining the tracks. I had to clean the bridge, the semaphore, the mountain, the station and station furniture, the village complete with homes, store fronts, trees and lamp posts, and numerous lead figures, animals as well as people.

When the cleaning was over and we'd cleaned ourselves, we moved the whole lot to the library.

Elena cleared the huge desk of the piles of books, and we laid down the tracks. Then she put the transformer on the desk, the electrical cord into the extension cord, and clipped the two thin wires connected to the front of the transformer to the tracks. Next, all three of us added the accessories and the figures. Finally, Elena placed the shiny black steam locomotive on the tracks, and the High Priest and I added the freight cars, the gondola, and the caboose.

It was ready to go!

Elena wheeled the desk chair, now stacked high with books, over to the desk, picked me up, and set me on top of the books.

"You can't stay on the desk while the train is running. And this is just the perfect height for you." Then she announced, "All aboard!"

She was about to turn on the transformer when I asked her if I might do it. She agreed, despite the High Priest's jealous protest. She explained that first I had to turn the knob all the way to the right so the electricity would go to the tracks. That's when the locomotive's head light and the light in the caboose would come on. To make the train move, I had to turn the knob all the way back to off and then again to the right. I had to do this slowly so the train wouldn't go too fast and derail.

And so, with baited breath, I turned the knob.

But no lights came on.

"You must have done it wrong," said the jealous High Priest.

Elena checked the wiring, I turned the knob again, and again nothing happened. After we tried several more times with the same result, she uttered a few colorful curses, then decided the fault was most certainly with the transformer. The next morning it was sent somewhere out of state to be repaired.

By the time it came back, days later, Elena was in the midst of shopping for the trip. The High Priest promised he'd hook the transformer up, but true to form, he never got around to it, and the unopened box has been sitting on the desk ever since.

Why don't I hook up the transformer myself? I'll surprise him. After all, he has a surprise for me for dinner, and one surprise deserves another.

I jump on the desk, slice the tape sealing the cardboard box with my claws, and take the transformer out. It's heavier than I thought, but giving up is out of the question. With considerable effort, I place it where Elena did, near the edge of the desk. I fasten the clips to the tracks and insert the plug into the extension cord . . . which is hanging from the arm of the desk chair.

Hmm. I don't remember anybody plugging the extension cord into the outlet when we set up the electric train.

Did Elena tell me to do it?

I now recall something to that effect. But then she promised to make fresh popcorn for us to eat while watching the train in motion. The thought of buttery popcorn knocked everything else out of my mind.

Oh, for the love of Bastet, I dread to think what Elena would say to me—nothing good for sure—if she found out I'd made her waste money to repair a perfectly good transformer.

I get on the floor and follow the extension cord under the desk to the outlet. I plug the cord in, crawl back to the chair, climb up, and sit on the pile of books Elena has conveniently left.

"All aboard!" I cry, then follow her instructions to a tee.

Slowly, the train leaves the station. The semaphore at the crossing turns from green to red, and the gate comes down to stop cars. When the train has passed, the light turns green again and the gate is lifted. Wonderful!

But there's no smoke coming out of the locomotive.

I remember Elena using an eyedropper to take a small amount of liquid from a little bottle and put it in the smoke stack. She said the liquid was resin and would turn into smoke once the train was in motion.

Maybe she didn't use enough resin. Luckily, the little bottle is still here on the desk. I stop the train, then, dispensing with the eyedropper, pour resin into the smoke stack and restart the train.

It passes a field of cows, climbs up the mountain, disappears into the tunnel, and reappears on the other side of the mountain. But still no smoke.

I'm about to give up hope when smoke begins to come out of the stack in small puffs. Soon the little locomotive is shooting smoke like the steam locomotives I've seen in old movies on TV. So realistic! It's beautiful to see the train pass through the village, leaving a trail of smoke behind. What a marvelous invention this is!

The smell of the smoke makes me I feel as if I were in a pine forest. So soothing. And the noise the train makes. So rhythmic, so hypnotic. Tatatata, tatatata . . . I can't keep my eyes open . . . tatatata, tatatata . . . I'm dozing off . . .

"What the hell is going on?"

The rude remark has a familiar voice.

The High Priest yells at me to turn the train off.

I open my eyes. He's audible, but not visible because the library is filled with smoke.

I feel fresh air rushing into the room and hear heavy footsteps moving toward me, followed by a loud crash and curses even more colorful than those Elena used when the train didn't work.

The room clears of smoke. The High Priest is massaging his right foot. The entire train, along with the transformer and most of the tracks, is on the floor.

After a series of accusations on his part and protestations of innocence on mine, we agree that the excess smoke was caused by a fault in the locomotive. We also agree to put the electric train set back in the boxes and return them to the attic. By the time Elena comes home she will have forgotten all about the electric train.

The High Priest decrees the work will be done after dinner, and since dinner isn't ready, I should employ my time by separating the tracks still on the table.

Limping slightly and cursing heavily, he leaves the library to return to his culinary tasks, and I start on the tracks.

The little bottle of resin is still on the desk. There's a warning printed on the label—faint, but still readable. "The locomotive has to be in motion for several minutes before it'll produce smoke. Do not overuse the resin because this will create excess smoke."

Sharing this information with the High Priest would only remind him of his painful foot. So I toss the bottle into the waste paper basket and go back to separating the tracks—

Smoke! I smell smoke!

But this time it isn't in the library. I rush out of the room, follow the smell to its source in the kitchen, and find the High Priest holding a smoking oven mitten under an open faucet.

"What happened?"

"A minor setback. Nothing to worry about. Everything is under control."

I hope Elena will tell us we can leave tomorrow. If we spend another day on our own in the house, there'll be no house.

"What are we having for dinner?"

"We were having lasagna."

"That's great. But why did you say 'were'?"

"I am afraid the lasagna has gone the way of the mitten."

"I see."

We have to leave tomorrow!

"What about scrambled eggs?" the High Priest asks apologetically. "Would you like that?"

"With bacon?"

"Of course."

"Count me in!"

Chapter 8

It's morning and I'm still in bed when I hear the phone ringing downstairs. I hope the High Priest will answer it, but he doesn't. He's probably turning over in his bed, waiting for the ringing to stop.

Then I remember that Elena is supposed to call us, and I'm downstairs in a flash. "Hello, hello," I yell into the receiver.

"Oh, thank God. I was beginning to think some catastrophe had befallen you two."

Remembering last night, I swallow hard before replying. "I'm sorry. I was still in bed."

"I have good news."

"Yes?"

"I've found a suitable place for the boat to dock. But where is Gato-Hamen?"

Good question.

"I don't know."

I feel a tap on my shoulder. It scares the life—one of the proverbial nine—out of me. I was so excited by Elena's good news I didn't hear the High Priest approaching.

"Make some noise when you come into a room," I say when I find my breath again.

"What do you mean?" asks Elena.

"Nothing, nothing. I was talking to Gato-Hamen."

"You just told me you didn't know where he was."

"Well, I found him."

"Let me speak to him."

I give the receiver to the sleepy High Priest, then, as before, jump onto the table and get up on my hind legs so I can put my ear close to the receiver.

"Hello, Elena," the High Priest says.

"Oh, hello, dear. I was just telling Puss in Boat that I've found a safe place for you to dock the boat."

"Where?"

"In the attic of the house where I'm staying."

"Are you sure it is safe?"

"No one goes up there. I know because it's covered in spider webs."

"Wonderful. We will leave when you tell us."

"Now would be fine."

"As soon as we prepare the boat."

"I'll be waiting for you." Elena makes kissing noises, then hangs up.

As the High Priest puts the receiver down, I jump to the floor.

"You told Elena we're almost ready to go. So you've composed a prayer to launch the boat?"

"I have been working on one."

"So it's not ready?"

"Now that Elena has told me where we can dock, I will be able to complete the prayer. It is just a question of a few more words."

"Maybe we should go to the library and uncover the boat."

"Good idea."

When we remove the sheets, the air is soon filled with dust, and some of the particles settle on my whiskers. Afraid of raising more dust, we don't attempt to fold the sheets, but just pile them in a corner for Elena to take care of one day.

The boat looks unchanged. If it could talk, I know what it would say. "It's about time you uncovered me. I'm ready for a new adventure."

"I will go upstairs to get my luggage," the High Priest says.

I remind him to bring my iron medallion down with him. I won't leave without the precious gift the Pharaoh gave me back in ancient Egypt.

In a few minutes, the High Priest returns with a piece of luggage in each hand and the medallion sticking out of one of his pants pockets. After depositing the luggage in the boat, he puts the chain with the medallion around my neck.

I wait for him to tell me what to do, but he's silent, his eyebrows knitted in concentration.

Is he putting the finishing touches to his prayer?

"Wrappa-Hamen, get aboard!" he says suddenly.

The prayer must be ready. I jump in the boat and enter the small cabin. The High Priest steps into the boat and begins to chant.

The dust from the sheets has gone from my whiskers to my nose. I try to hold back a sneeze by putting a paw over it, but it's no use. I sneeze hard and loud!

The chanting stops. I move further into the cabin, but not before getting a look of disapproval for the interruption.

The High Priest resumes chanting, and as usual the boat begins to rock, then spin. When he's finished, he hurries inside the cabin, and the boat spins faster and faster.

Are we going to lose consciousness as we did on the other trips?

Chapter 9

I wake up in a daze. I leave the cabin, and a refreshing cool breeze clears my mind. The High Priest is standing at the bow, staring straight ahead. I stand upright and follow his gaze.

Two things are certain. It's dawn, and we aren't in an attic.

"Look," he says calmly. "It is the beginning of a new day."

"Yes, but we aren't in an attic."

"I know that."

"What went wrong?"

"I can only surmise. I think your sneeze caused my prayer to go awry."

"Are you saying it's my fault?"

"Well, it was, indirectly."

Typical! The High Priest can't admit he screwed up. I'd like to give him a direct kick in the shin.

"But where are we?"

"On a road in an open plain."

He's hopeless. I'll have to try figure out where we are by studying our surroundings.

The day's first sunrays illuminate the wide white road where our boat has landed. On each side of the road is a large earth mound covered in white chalk. The mounds glimmer in the light, like two giant sugar cakes, and despite our predicament, the sight of them makes me hungry. The white road leads to a circular stone building made up of a series of arches.

I pull on the High Priest's sleeve and point to it.

"For the love of the gods, I know this building," he announces, excited. "I have seen it before, but where, where?" He takes a deep breath, scratches his head, then exhales loudly through his mouth. "I have it. Of course!"

"You know where we are then?"

"Yes."

"Are you going to tell me?"

"Yes, yes. You must forgive me. I am just very surprised. We are in Stonehenge . . . My prayer worked, to an extent."

"To an extent? To what extent?! We aren't in an attic, and Elena is nowhere to be seen."

"True, but we are in Stonehenge, and Stonehenge, like Bath, is in England."

The High Priest looks guilty, like someone who's hiding something.

"Is there something else you want to tell me?"

"Well . . . we are a few years short of the correct date, just a bit off the mark."

I'm afraid to ask, but I have to. "How many years?"

"I would say 3000 to 3,500 thousand years."

My legs go weak. I have to hold myself up by leaning against the side of the boat.

"You mean we're in ancient England—1500 to 1000 B.C.?"

He nods. I sigh.

"How do you know about Stonehenge?"

"Remember the night Elena showed us a tourist guide to England?"

"I remember. I fell asleep."

"While you were napping, I was studying. What you see in front of you was built in stages over more than a thousand years. Unless my memory fails me, we are looking at the final product, which is believed to have been completed at about 1500 BC. But, of course, only when I see the inside can I be certain."

So the High Priest plans to play tourist, while poor Elena, covered in spider webs, is in an attic worrying about our whereabouts.

I'm about to tell him how selfish he is when two powerful hands take hold of me, pinning my forelegs against my body.

"Help!"

But the High Priest is in no position to help anyone. A tall, strongly built, mean-looking man in a white robe is holding a sharp-looking dagger to his throat.

I look around. The boat is surrounded by men also wearing white robes, each with a dagger in his belt.

They start to yell at us. It's a guttural language—not very pretty, just like these men. I don't understand what they're saying, but I think they want us out of the boat.

I'm right. The man holding me lifts me out of the boat and plants me on the ground. He loosens his grip slightly and I manage to bite him on the hand.

"Assassin!" I scream.

He lets me go, but takes his dagger from his belt and points it at my belly.

Suddenly I'm no longer hungry. In fact, I don't think I'll ever be hungry again.

The man holding a dagger to the High Priest's throat forces him out of boat and shoves him in the direction of the building he called Stonehenge.

Then it's my turn to get shoved. I'm made to walk behind him, the dagger now at my back. The rest of the men trail behind us.

Is this any way to treat visitors?

As we walk down the wide white road towards Stonehenge, we pass between the two large sugar cakes, then between two large stones and, at the end of the road, two more. We enter a circular field surrounded by a deep ditch with a high bank on its inner side. In middle of the field stands Stonehenge.

What sort of place is this? It has no roof, so it can't be a building where people live. Is it the equivalent of an Egyptian pyramid? Is this sacred ground? Did we commit some sacrilege by coming here?

I fear the worst.

We go down the path that crosses the field and enter Stonehenge through one of the arches. Straight ahead, in an enormous horseshoe of stones, stands a tall man. Like our captors, he's wearing a white robe, but he also has a black hood. With his back to us, he's standing directly in front of what looks like an altar.

We stop walking. One of our captors goes up to the man with the black hood and whispers in his ear. He must be telling him about the man who wears strange clothing and has an even stranger companion, a cat who talks and walks upright.

When he's finished his report, he steps away from the man with the black hood, who raises a hand wielding a knife.

Are those animal legs I see stretched on the altar?

I shiver. I know what's going to happen next. The hand plunges down, mercilessly, and a scream of pain echoes throughout Stonehenge.

In the silence that follows, I swallow hard. The High Priest and I exchange glances. He looks as frightened as I am.

The man in the black hood turns. He wears a golden mask covering the top half of his face. He still holds the sacrificial knife. It's covered with blood, and there are large blood stains on the front of his white robe.

Wait! It isn't a man at all, but a woman! The contours of her breasts show under her robe. She's looking in my direction. Am I going to be the next victim?

She's not looking at me, but past me. Our captors turn and look in the same direction, and the High Priest and I turn to see what everyone is looking at. It's one of the most wondrous things I've seen in my life. The sun has risen above the horizon and now sits like a radiant giant orange on top of the single stone near the gate.

Are the people of this land sun-worshippers, and is the slaughtered animal an offering? Am I going to be the next animal to be sacrificed?

"It is definitely the later stages of building," the High Priest says.

Why is he telling this when I'm about to be sacrificed? If he's trying to get my mind off my impending death, he's failed.

His comment has gotten the woman's attention. She stares at him, drops the knife, and says something to the congregation. Because of the mask, I can't tell her expression, but from her tone of voice it seems she's angry.

Everyone leaves except the two men guarding us with daggers, and the woman walks towards us.

I fear we're in big trouble. Why couldn't the High Priest keep his mouth shut?

The woman stops in front of me and looks at the medallion on my chest.

"Leave him alone," the High Priest says.

"You are Egyptians. This," she says, lifting my medallion gently with her hand, "confirms it."

I understand what she's saying because she's now speaking in Egyptian.

She yanks the chain. "They tell me you talk," she says, fixing her eyes on mine. "Then talk!"

I clear my throat. "Yes, we're Egyptians. We weren't supposed to come here. It was a mistake. A mistake made by the High Priest," I add, hoping to shift her attention to him.

"He sneezed," he says. "That threw my prayer off."

"Stop babbling, you two. You had better say something that makes sense."

If she expects the High Priest to make sense, we're in big trouble! I've been waiting for that day myself, and I don't think it'll be today.

Maybe if I tell her our story it'll take her mind off sacrificing me.

"I was a stray cat, back in ancient Egypt," I begin. "One day in a looted tomb I was kicked by a man who turned out to be the Vizier. Purely in self-defense, I spat a cat amulet at him, hitting him on the forehead, and he accused me of trying to kill him. The man you see before you was, is, the High Priest of Amun-Ra. When he heard the commotion, he came into the tomb . . ."

I get as far as describing how the Pharaoh, seeing me walk and talk like a human being, laughed for the first time since his parents' death, when I have to stop to catch my breath.

"Stop!" the woman says when I try to continue. "Let us go to my home. You can finish your story there."

She gestures to the two men to withdraw their daggers, and, with a movement of her head, dismisses them.

"Come."

We follow her to the rear of Stonehenge and then out into the surrounding field. As we walk, I wonder about the chalky mounds, some quite large, almost hill-like, that lie all around. Are they tombs, like our pyramids?

We enter a forest, and once in a while the woman turns to make sure we're still behind her. The sunrays hardly penetrate the thick foliage. It seems as if night has fallen. We walk for fifteen or twenty minutes before we reach a circular wooden house. Smoke is rising from an opening in the thatched roof.

"Here we are. My home."

She pushes the door open. A man is crouching by a fire burning in the middle of the room.

"Tara," she calls.

Tara gets up and walks toward us. He's very tall and quite broad in the chest and shoulders. The bare forearms sticking out of the sleeves of his robe are knotted with muscle. He bows to the woman, who removes her black hood and hands it to him.

Her hair is dark and luxuriant and falls to her shoulders. The black cord attached to either end of her golden mask, which she makes no attempt to remove, is almost invisible.

"We have visitors," she tells Tara in Egyptian. "You had better prepare some food."

He straightens up. "Yes, mistress. It will be done," he replies in Egyptian.

"So there are other Egyptians here?" the High Priest asks.

"No, I am the only one. I have taught Tara our language."

Then he asks the question I've been dying to ask since we met her. "How do you happen to be here?"

Silence.

But he's undeterred. "Well, at least answer this. Are you the high priestess of the temple?"

A high priestess, like Norma in the opera . . .

"Yes, but now ask no more questions. I want to hear the rest of your story."

The High Priest has met his match, someone as stubborn as he is.

There's a large bench covered in sheepskin near the circular clay hearth where logs burn in a metal grate with cloven hooves. The High Priestess goes over to it and sits down.

"Sit," she tells me, and I obey.

How I wish she would take the golden mask off so I can see her entire face. Looking at her long thin neck, her full lips, and her dark soulful eyes, I surmise she is a beautiful woman.

"Are you going to remove your mask?"

"As High Priestess, I do not show my face to anyone."

She motions to the High Priest to join us. He sits on her other side.

"Continue your story," she says to me.

I tell her how the Pharaoh took me to live with him at court and describe our year together, where we went, what we said to each other. "The Vizier so resented our relationship he poisoned the Pharaoh and accused me of the murder. I escaped death thanks to the High Priest here who took me away from Egypt on a magic boat. We arrived in a city called New York thousands of years in the future—"

"A tiny miscalculation on my part," interjects the High Priest.

"So you can journey through time?"

"To an extent."

I'm about to resume my story when Tara comes back carrying a wooden tray that he lays down on a table in front of our bench. There are three wooden spoons and three wooden bowls filled to the rim with milk on which berries float. The sight of this delicacy has revived my appetite, and I begin to salivate. Tara hands a bowl to each of us, then a spoon. We wait for the High Priestess to start, and as soon as she does, we join her.

The buttery milk has retained the warmth of the cow's udder, and the berries taste freshly picked. Living in New York City has made me forget what fresh fruit tastes like. It's wonderful! I'm the first to finish.

I'm licking my whiskers when the High Priestess asks me, "So what happened in the city you call New York?"

I tell her about Elena and the ancient spell that could revive the dead, how the High Priest retrieved it from her memory using the Entering, how we then returned to ancient Egypt to revive the Pharaoh, and how when the High Priest recited the spell over his mummy, it didn't work.

I stop for few seconds because I know what I'm about to tell the High Priestess will shock her.

"Then the cat-goddess Bastet appeared to us and said she had given me my powers. She asked me if I was willing to sacrifice my life to bring the Pharaoh back from the dead . . ."

My mouth has become dry with emotion. I ask the High Priestess if I might have more milk. She turns to Tara and nods, and he brings me another bowl, which I quickly drain.

"I believe he's getting tired," the High Priest says. "Maybe I should tell the rest of the story."

I am tired, and the fire's warmth is making me drowsy.

"Go on," the High Priestess says.

"He told Bastet he was willing to sacrifice his life. But she said he did not have to trade his life for the Pharaoh's. His willingness to sacrifice himself would make the spell work. Then Bastet rewarded him with two further gifts—longevity and the ability to write. She vanished, and the Pharaoh came back to life . . ."

The High Priest describes how Egypt had suffered a great deal when the Vizier usurped the throne, and how after the Pharaoh regained his strength he defeated the Vizier's army, killed him, and went back to governing his people. "But not for long. The Pharaoh had to leave his beloved cat and return to the world above . . ."

I start to sob. The High Priestess picks me up and puts me on her lap.

"You are a big cat."

I rub my face on her robe to dry my tears. Forgetting my bandaged wound, I start to nestle my head against her and cry out in pain. She gently pets me, as if consoling a child.

"I meant to ask you about your head. What happened to you?"

"I got hurt saving the High Priest."

It's not really a lie. If I hadn't forced my head through the window, we wouldn't have gotten back inside to answer the phone when Elena called from the airport, and she would have returned home suspecting something was wrong, found us outside, and . . . I did save the High Priest—I saved him from Elena.

"You are a brave cat. You were willing to sacrifice your life for the Pharaoh, and then later risk it for your friend."

I'm purring shamelessly. I turn over onto my back so I can look into her eyes, and she strokes me on the belly.

"How sad that you lost the Pharaoh again."

"But I haven't . . . Seven years after he left another war broke out. This one was lost. The High Priest and I returned to New York City only to find we were the same age we had been when we left. For Elena, only five months had gone by, but she was different in one way. She was pregnant with the High Priest's child. The smell of blue lotus, the unmistakable odor of my beloved Pharaoh, emanated from her belly . . . He was to be reborn. He's now one year old."

"You are a fortunate cat as well as a brave one," the High

Priestess says.

"Now that you know our story, will you not tell us yours?" the High Priest asks.

"Mine is a story no one should hear."

"You are as stubborn as a donkey. But will you at least answer some questions about the temple where we were earlier?"

"If I can."

"In the future, the temple is known as Stonehenge. What do you call it?"

"God's Stone."

"Is it true God's Stone is some kind of calendar?"

The High Priestess laughs for the first time.

I like her laughter. It's sincere, just like Elena's.

And in the firelight her lips are the color of sun-dried bricks, just like Elena's, and her teeth sparkle like Elena's . . . Oh, poor Elena! She must be sick with worry.

"Why do you laugh?" asks the High Priest, annoyed.

"It is amusing to think of God's Stone as some kind of calendar."

"You mean it is not?"

"I did not say that. But God's Stone is so much more."

"Will you tell me what its significance is?"

"I am the High Priestess of God's Stone. You are asking me to betray my vows. You, a high priest, should know better. Would you ever reveal your secret knowledge to one of the uninitiated?"

"I see your point, but—"

The High Priest doesn't get to finish. Tara has returned, his long shadow stretching over us. He's carrying the High Priestess's black hood.

"It is time," he says.

Time for what? Is she going back to God's Stone to sacrifice another animal? Me?

"Don't worry," she says as if reading my thoughts. "You are both free to go."

She lifts me off her lap and sets me on the ground, then takes the black hood from Tara, puts it on, and stands up.

"I must be going."

The High Priest also gets up. Tara holds the door open for us, bows to us as we leave, and gives me a big smile, which I reciprocate.

As before, the High Priestess leads the way, but her pace is quicker now. It's clear she's in a hurry. I'm right behind her with the High Priest in the rear. I have to get down on my fours to keep up, and I hear him huffing and puffing behind me. And to think that he's always telling me I should lose weight!

The High Priestess's white robe gets caught in the bushes again and again, but she never stops. She just pulls the robe away, at one point tearing it. Finally, we're out of the forest and in the field we crossed earlier. God's Stone is but a few hundred paces away.

"Hurry," she tells us.

We're no longer just walking fast, but running. She takes us through God's Stone, across the field on the other side, and down the wide white road to our boat.

"You must go before the men who captured you come back. I am sure they have told the king about you.

"King? What king?" asks the High Priest.

"Did you not realize there would be a king to govern this land? He will want to sacrifice the talking cat tomorrow on Midsummer Day."

I'm glad this king wasn't there when the magic boat appeared. As for "the talking cat," I have a name, and I want the High Priestess to know it.

"My name is Wrappa-Hamen."

"What a beautiful name. And the High Priest? What is your name?"

"Permit me to introduce myself. I am Gato-Hamen."

When the High Priestess doesn't compliment him on his name, he looks hurt and she notices. "An interesting name."

The High Priest and I board the boat and stand in the bow.

"I will stay until you leave."

"You haven't told us your name," I say.

"Nor will I."

It's become gusty, and the black hood is blown from her head. Her dark hair rises above her shoulders, fluttering. Men in white robes, daggers in hand, are running in our direction.

55

The High Priest, unable to speak from fear, points at them.

She turns and sees them. "Go."

"What about you?" he manages to say. "The men will surely tell the king you let us go."

"Do not worry about me. I will be all right. But now you must go. Go!"

"Farewell then, nameless, noble High Priestess." She nods her head.

"I'll never forget you," I add.

"Nor I you, Wrappen-Hamen."

The High Priest begins chanting the same prayer he did in New York. The men are getting closer. I don't know if he sees them, for he's chanting fervently.

I hope there are no problems!

The men are about fifty paces from us. I poke the the High Priest to get him to hasten his chanting. He does, and the boat begins to rock and spin.

Before I go into the cabin, I look back. The men have reached the boat, but the whirlwind created by the spinning casts them to the ground. The High Priestess stands where she was, the sides of her white robe rising like angel's wings in what seems a gesture of protection.

Chapter 10

When I wake up, I'm not in the boat, but lying on a cold floor near the bow. What's this on my nose? Yuck, a spider. I brush it off.

I get up and take in my surroundings. I'm in an attic, hopefully the right attic. But where's Elena? And for that matter, where's the High Priest?

I hear moaning coming from behind the boat and go to have a look. He's also been thrown from the boat and is lying on the floor. I get down on all fours and lick his face.

"Oh, Wrappa-Hamen. Did the spell work this time?"

"I think so. Let's explore." With some difficulty, the High Priest gets up. I look him up and down. He seems normal. Maybe in his case "normal" is going too far, but he's standing.

The attic is dark except for the moonlight coming in through two small windows. There are old trunks and pieces of furniture covered in dust and spider webs, just as Elena told us.

"Shouldn't Elena be here?" I ask.

"Maybe when we did not appear, she went to sleep."

Typical Elena behavior!

"Are we going to tell her you made a mistake and took us to the past?"

"How many times must I tell you? I did not make a mistake. You sneezed and threw my prayer off . . . And of course we are going to tell her!"

"Fine."

"Fine." The High Priest always likes to have the last word.

"Fine," I say under my breath.

"By the way, you do realize you have met a high priestess just as I told you you would."

"For the love of the gods, you're right. But you also told me she would reveal secrets to me. How do you account for the fact she didn't?"

"Hmm, I cannot. But take heed."

At times like these, I need all my self-control not to scratch him.

"Shouldn't we get out of this attic and look for Elena?" I ask.

"I guess so."

"Fine."

"Fine."

This time I let him have the last word.

"Follow me."

I walk over to the door. Just as I turn the knob, I hear a crashing sound behind me, like a cascade of metal objects. I turn around. The High Priest is massaging his knee, and scattered on the floor around his feet are forty or fifty pieces of flatware. Also on the floor is the box that contained them.

"Do you think you could make more noise?" I say.

Forgetting my feline ears are far more sensitive than human ones, he curses under his breath, using profanities even I didn't know existed.

I pull the door open a few inches, just enough to stick my head out. There's a small landing and a flight of stair leading to the floor below. I listen. All's quiet. I hope the High Priest lets it stay that way.

I open the door wider, step out onto the landing, and whisper to him to follow. The area is in darkness. No problem for me, but I'm concerned about the High Priest.

"Hold on to my tail," I tell him and extend it so he can grab it.

Nothing happens. I turn around to see what the problem is, but he isn't there—

Suddenly, a bright light is shining in my eyes! I'm stunned. I lose my footing, tumble down the stairs, and land on my rump.

Dazed, I hear footsteps on the stairs above me. Then the High Priest is standing over me, shaking me. "Wrappa-Hamen, Wrappa-Hamen, are you all right?"

"I think I'll survive—that is, if you stop doing that. What the hell was that light?"

"It was me. I went back into the room to get a flashlight I saw in there." He has the gall to switch it back on and shine it in my eyes again!

Now it's my turn to curse at him, and I use profanities I'm sure he's never heard before! Between one curse and another, I manage to tell him to switch the damn thing off.

After I regain my self-control, I check myself for broken

bones. Everything seems intact, except for my dignity.

When I get up, I smell roast chicken.

Is the shock from the fall making me hallucinate?

No. The smell is too good to be imaginary.

I realize I'm starving. I ate only a few hours ago at Stonehenge, but, technically, I haven't eaten in more than three thousands years. I have to find the source of the delicious smell.

We're on a small landing, and a second flight of stairs leads to a lower floor. I have no problem seeing, but I fear the High Priest might have another accident.

"Now's the time to turn on the flashlight. But please don't point it at me!" I hear several clicks, but see no light. "What's the matter?"

"Well, er, the flashlight no longer works. The batteries are probably dead."

Unable to see, he might break his neck before I find the roast chicken. I'm sorely tempted to leave him behind, but if I run into Elena she'll be angry with me for deserting him. We'll both have to rely on my night vision. "Grab my tail, and don't let go."

This time he takes it and holds it tightly in a sweaty hand. The discomfort I feel verges on pain, but I'm willing to bear it since it means knowing where the maniac is at all times.

As we go down the stairs, the smell of roast chicken grows stronger. The stairs seem interminable. When we finally reach the bottom, we find ourselves in a small corridor. The smell is coming from behind one of the doors.

I push it open. It's a kitchen! It has a large window through which I see only a stone wall until I crane my neck and look up. On top of the wall is a railing, and between the bars I can see pieces of the moon-lit sky. The kitchen is in the basement of the house.

There's enough light for the High Priest to see by. He lets go of my tail. I give it a comforting lick and him a dirty look.

The kitchen is double the size of our kitchen in New York. In the middle is a massive wooden table. I jump up on it in hope of finding the roast chicken, but I'm disappointed. All I find are a bowl of fruit, a pitcher of water, and an open bottle of red wine.

I hear the familiar sound of a refrigerator's generator kicking in. Is the roast chicken in the refrigerator?

"Why are we here?" the High Priest asks.

"That question man has been asking himself since the beginning of time."

"Wrappa-Hamen, you know very well what I mean."

"I thought I smelled Elena."

"Well, she is not here. We should search the house for her."

He can be very annoying. To leave now, when I'm so close to that roast chicken, would be pure insanity.

I decide to ignore him and jump down from the table to look for the refrigerator. I find it, open the door, and, inside, illuminated by the bulb, sits the object of my desire. It's on a large plate, surrounded by roast potatoes, carrots and onions.

Carefully, I take the plate out with my forepaws and set it on the table. I don't want another noisy accident, so I leave the refrigerator open to give the High Priest more light.

"Mm, that roast chicken looks good. Do you think we could each have a piece?"

That's what I thought he would say.

"What about Elena?"

"She can wait."

That's what I thought he would say.

Someone has already gotten to the wings. I pull a leg off for myself, then remove the other one and hand it to the High Priest.

"Exquisite," he says after taking a bite.

I agree—whoever cooked this chicken knows his business! "What about some wine?"

"Good idea. Let me find some glasses."

"Don't bother. We can drink from the bottle."

I grab it from the table, hand it to him, and he takes a long sip. "Ah, blood of the gods," he says, returning the bottle to me.

I'm drinking the wine when the kitchen door swings open and a ghost enters. It has wires in its head and is wearing a long white robe. I spit out the wine, spraying the table and the High Priest. The bottle falls from my paws, crashing loudly as it hits the floor. I leap on the High Priest's head and close my eyes.

The ghost speaks. "What the hell are you doing?!"

Funny. The ghost speaks in Elena's voice.

I open one eye. It is Elena!

"What's that on your head?" I ask.

"Hair pins. What's that on your head?" She points to my bandage. "And what happened to you two? I waited in the attic for hours for the boat to appear."

She walks over to the refrigerator and slams the door closed, leaving only moonlight to see by.

I hear muffled sounds from under my rump. Oops. It's the High Priest. I carefully crawl down from his head to his shoulder. He spits out some fur I must've shed out of fear.

"We encountered some turbulence," he says.

Elena draws a chair and sits at the table. "Hold that thought. Now tell me, Wrappa-Hamen, what happened to your head?"

I swallow hard before answering. "I was cleaning a windowsill when the window came down on my head. Gato-Hamen stitched me up."

"I see," Elena says, arching one eyebrow. "Now you, sit," she commands the High Priest. "What do you mean you were delayed by turbulence?"

Glad her anger is no longer directed at me, I breathe a sigh of relief. But she adds, looking in my direction, "And don't you move from his shoulder."

I have no intention of going anywhere, but if I did I would certainly have to give it up now. Sometimes I think Elena could have been a general.

And so the inquisition, made more threatening by near darkness, begins.

"I asked you," she says to the High Priest, "what do you mean you were delayed by turbulence?"

I feel sorry for him—that is, until he tells Elena the "turbulence" was my sneezing during his prayer. I make sure he knows I'm displeased by digging a claw into his shoulder. After a loud "ouch," he goes on to describe what happened to us in Stonehenge.

Elena punctuates his narrative with "incredible" or "unbelievable." When he finishes, she begins her relentless questioning. Every last detail must be recounted, and I step in whenever the High Priest's memory falters.

Inevitably, she asks me, "When Gato-Hamen read the Tarot cards, didn't he say you would meet a high priestess who would reveal secrets to you?"

"I know, I know. But she didn't reveal anything."

Elena looks at the High Priest. "How do you explain that?"

"I cannot. But I can tell you this—I have never misread a man's future. Granted, he is a cat, but still."

"Look, you two," I say. "It's my future, and I don't want to talk about it. Now, can we return to the present?"

I jump from the High Priest's shoulder onto the table. "Elena, I've been dying to ask you, who was the cook who prepared this sublime chicken?"

"That would be John. He's the factotum here. He's a wonderful man."

The High Priest grimaces. "Oh, really? So where is this wonderful man?"

I'm going to stay out of this one. Elena once told me an Italian proverb, "*Tra moglie e marito non mettere dito.*" "Don't come between husband and wife." I finish my chicken leg and listen to their marital tiff.

"John is asleep, I suppose," Elena replies.

"Still? With all the noise we made?"

"He must be a heavy sleeper, like me. I didn't hear you either. Of course, I wouldn't have heard you even if I had been awake. You came down the servants' staircase."

"If the noise we made didn't wake you up, why are you here?" I ask, even though I think I know the answer.

She hesitates. "Er, my stomach woke me up."

That's what I thought. And she had the gall to scare the hell out of us when we were doing exactly what she had planned to do.

"But I think we should call it a night. We're going to get up early tomorrow."

"Why?" the High Priest and I ask in unison.

"Because tomorrow there's a flea market here in Bath."

"Fleas? You want to buy fleas?" I ask, not believing what I just heard.

"Oh, Puss in Boat, you can be so silly sometimes. A flea market is where you buy old things, used things, antiques."

"But why is it called a flea market?"

"Oh, I don't know exactly. I guess it's because old clothing is sometimes flea-ridden. But I don't think we'll encounter any fleas."

"I see."

But I don't see. I don't like fleas, and why anyone would risk catching them is beyond me.

Elena gets up, goes to the switch by the kitchen door to turn the lights on, then walks over to the table, picks up the plate with the chicken, and, much to my dismay, puts it back in the refrigerator.

She goes into a cupboard, takes out a broom and a palette, hands them to the High Priest, and points to the pieces of glass on the floor. "You'd better clean this mess up. I don't want John to see it."

He bites his bottom lip—I wonder what curse he's suppressing.

"And you," she says, looking at me and handing me a sponge she took from the sink, "you'd better clean the table."

I do some lip-biting of my own as I take the sponge.

"That's better," she says when we've finished with our chores. Why is she pointing an index finger at me? What's she does she have in mind now? "Remember, Wrappa-Hamen, in this house you must act like a normal cat."

"Normal?"

"You know exactly what I mean," she says, fixing her gaze on me. "No walking or talking like a human, or doing anything else for that matter that resembles human behavior. Do we understand each other?"

"Yes, ma'am!" I say, while bowing. "Does that mean I don't get a bedroom to myself?"

"Yes. I mean, no, you don't."

"I see. You mean I'll have to sleep on a pillow on a chair?"

"That's what normal cats do."

This English vacation may not yield the pleasures I'd anticipated.

"I almost forgot about your medallion," Elena adds. "I'm sorry. You can't wear it here. You'd better take it off and give it to me."

I oblige, and she puts it in her robe pocket and gives me a comforting pet on my head. "Thank you, Wrappa-Hamen. I promise to take good care of it."

She opens the kitchen door. "Quietly, now," she says before stepping through with the High Priest behind her and me in the rear.

We climb the servants' staircase. On the first landing, she points to a door. "This leads to the ground floor rooms," she whispers. "We're going to the first floor. That's where our bedroom is."

"Isn't this the first floor?" I ask.

"Not in England," she explains. "Here the ground floor is, well, the ground floor. The next floor is the first floor."

We climb another flight of stairs to another door, which she opens. "Follow as quietly as you can," she whispers.

The floor isn't carpeted. Elena is wearing slippers, but the High Priest is wearing sneakers, and they squeak with every step. She stops, turns around, and commands him to take them off.

We resume our walk like three thieves in the night, Elena tiptoeing gracefully, the High Priest ungracefully, with a sneaker dangling from each hand. I walk comfortably and soundlessly on my padded paws.

We pass a big staircase. "This is the main stairs," Elena informs us. "Our bedroom is that one." She points ahead of us to the left. "It faces the front. It has the most gorgeous view."

We're almost there when something hits me on the head!

Hurt and frightened, I give out a cry to wake the dead.

"Shush!" Elena commands.

"What the hell was that?" I ask, rubbing my head.

The High Priest bends down. "I'm afraid it was me," he says sheepishly. "I dropped one of my sneakers."

"Assassin," I cry.

"Shush," repeats Elena.

I hear someone running across the floor above us. She hears it, too. "Now you've done it. You've woken up John."

Within seconds, the famous John runs down the main stairs and appears by our side. He's barefooted and wearing a long striped nightgown. "Is everything all right, madam? I heard what sounded like a jaguar's cry."

"That was Leopold," Elena says.

The High Priest and I look around, searching for Leopold. Behind her back, Elena shakes an index finger at me.

I understand. For some unfathomable reason, I'm now Leopold.

John gives me an appraising look. "I see, madam. Not only does he make sounds like a jaguar, but he's as big as one. What unfortunate accident befell him that he had to be bandaged?"

The High Priest befell him. That's what!

"Oh, nothing serious," Elena assures him. "He received a minor scrape."

She sees John looking at the High Priest. "How silly of me, John. Let me introduce my husband, Jack."

The High Priest looks dumbstruck. It takes him a moment to realize he's Jack. "How do you do, John?"

"Fine, sir. How do you do? We were expecting you this afternoon."

"Their bo . . . I mean, his plane was late," Elena says.

"I'll fetch the luggage, madam."

"No, no!" cries Elena. Seeing John's puzzled look, she adds, "Jack has already brought it up."

"Very well, madam. Would madam and sir like to have a repast?"

"I took care of that, John. Thank you."

"Should I prepare something for Leopold?"

Good idea, John. I rub myself against his leg.

"No, he's on a diet."

Diet?

"I see," says John, looking me over.

"I'm afraid we've spoiled him."

If I were allowed to talk, I'd have a few things to say to Elena!

"Well, if madam and sir require nothing else, I'll bid you good night."

"Sorry we woke you up. Good night, John."

"Good night, madam, sir. Good night, Leopold." John bends down and runs a finger under my chin. I reply with a purr.

I watch him disappear up the stairs before turning to Elena. But she and the High Priest are down the corridor standing in front of a door. She's waving at me to follow.

"Where did you get a name like Leopold?" I ask her when I reach them.

"If you really must know, I named you after a character in the novel *Ulysses*."

In a few days I've gone from Wrappa-Hamen to Gastone to Leopold. I dread to think what my next name will be.

"Was there a character named Jack as well?" asks the High Priest.

"No. Jack is a very common name."

He looks displeased, but thinks better of complaining.

Elena opens the door. "Come, Gato-Hamen. This is our bedroom. Good night, Wrappa-Hamen."

Much to my dismay, they go inside and Elena closes the door behind them. Then it opens again.

Of course, she's pulling my leg!

Just as I'm about to go inside, she comes out holding a pillow, which she drops on a chair. "Good night, Leopold," she says as she closes the door.

Bloody hell!

I knock on the door, which opens an inch. "Stop making noise. You'll wake Alexander."

"I'm supposed to act normal, right?" I whisper. "Don't normal cats sleep with their people? So shouldn't I be sleeping in your bedroom?"

"Normal cats do sleep with their people," she whispers back before closing the door again. "But you, Wrappa-Hamen, are not a normal cat."

Elena can twist words to her advantage. Is she unique, or is this true of every woman?

Defeated, I climb on the chair, sit on the big white pillow, then lie down. Travel is exhausting, especially time travel. I wet a forepaw and rub myself down till sleep overcomes me . . .

I dream of the woman in the mirror. I don't see her, but I hear her. Her voice is muffled. I think she's asking for help.

"Tell me where you are," I say.

She falls silent, and my heart, which has been pounding wildly, begins to slow down. But just as it resumes its normal beat, I have another dream . . .

I'm back at Stonehenge. I'm in the boat, and the High Priestess is walking away from me on the wide white avenue leading to the temple. As when we left her, the wind ruffles her dark hair and white robe. The sun, high in the sky, is sending down enormous flares in the shape of hands, hands that hover over her as if blessing or protecting her.

I jump out of the boat and run after her. But as hard as I run, I never reach her.

Suddenly, she stops and turns. I don't know how, but I find myself by her side. She brings her hands to her face, and I see the blood pulsate in the blue veins beneath her thin skin. She's taking off her gold mask. Finally I'll get to see what she looks like . . .

Chapter 11

I'm awoken by a blow on the head.

What the hell was that? It seems to be open season on my poor head.

"I'm sorry, Leopold," John says apologetically. "I'm afraid I dropped a fork."

It's lying next to me on the big white pillow. John is standing over me holding a large serving tray with the palm of one hand. I smell fried eggs, hot chocolate, tea, coffee, toast, jam, marmalade, fried tomatoes, and, yes, bangers and baked beans.

With his other hand, John uncovers a dish, takes something from it, and hands to me. It's a beautiful, well-cooked banger!

"I know you're on a diet, but what madam doesn't see, madam doesn't know."

I don't stand on ceremony. I snatch it from his hand with my forepaw, devour it, then jump down from the chair and rub against his legs, going between and around them as if tracing a figure eight.

"That's a good cat. I'm forgiven for dropping a fork on your head, right?"

"Meeeooow."

John knocks on the bedroom door.

"Come in," Elena says.

Carefully carrying the tray, he turns the handle with his free hand, opens the door, and goes in. "Good morning, madam. Good morning, sir."

I sneak into the bedroom behind him. Elena and the High Priest are in bed. John puts the tray down on a round table by the window, then draws the curtains. Sunlight comes rushing in.

"What the . . . ?" the High Priest says in a sleepy voice. He doesn't get a chance to finish his curse because Elena elbows him in the side.

John sets the table for breakfast.

"Would madam like me to pour her tea?" he asks when he's finished.

"Thank you, John. I'll take care of it."

"As you wish, madam."

When John leaves, I ask Elena if it's all right to wake up the little Pharaoh, whose crib is next to her side of the big bed.

"Yes, of course. Alexander will be thrilled to see you. He's missed you."

I stand upright at the foot of the crib. The little Pharaoh is sleeping with a smile on his face.

What's he dreaming about? Pulling on my tail perhaps?

I stick it through the slats and tickle his little feet with the tip. He begins to laugh, and I'm brought back to ancient Egypt. I tickled his feet when I woke up in his bed for the first time. So much has happened since that day. Then, the Pharaoh was like a brother to me. I'm grateful to have him back as a child, but I can't help remembering him the way he was—

Pain brings me back to the present. The little Pharaoh is yanking on my tail! I pull myself free and jump onto the breakfast table, where Elena and the High Priest are sitting and sipping from thin white porcelain cups. I butter a piece of toast, take a spoonful of jam, and plop it on top.

Mmm. Delicious.

"Oh, really, Wrappa-Hamen," says Elena. "Where are your manners?"

"I'm a normal cat, remember?"

"Have you ever seen a normal cat butter himself a piece of toast and spread jam on it?" she asks the High Priest.

"No," he replies. After giving the matter more thought, he adds, "But then I have never seen a cat eat the way Wrappa-Hamen does."

"I give up," Elena says.

Good!

I stick a spoon into the bowl of baked beans and shovel a large helping into my mouth. Next I dig my claw into a banger, lift it to my mouth, and bite off a piece. Then I alternate between spoonfuls of baked beans and bites of the banger.

Delicious! Even Elena's disapproving looks can't dampen my appetite.

"That's enough," she says, taking me by the scruff of the neck and trying to lift me off the table—and I mean trying. She lets go of my neck. "Oh, hell, I can't budge him. He's too fat!"

With no hope that Elena will let me resume breakfast, I decide to take a look outside. I jump from the table to the windowsill. The window is open, and a light breeze runs through my fur, removing the last of the night's torpor.

Now fully awake, I look at the enchanting view. The house we're staying in is part of a group of houses set in a semicircle. The shape of the street and the green field across the road reminds me of Stonehenge with its stone circles and surrounding greenery.

"I can't wait to show you and Wrappa-Hamen the city," Elena says excitedly.

"I have just remembered," says the High Priest. "My clothing and his carrier bag are still in the attic."

"You can go and retrieve your stuff when John leaves for his morning jog."

My tail is being tugged again, and I turn to see the little Pharaoh sitting on Elena's lap, chewing happily. In one hand he holds my poor tail, in the other a half-eaten banger.

I hope he doesn't confuse them. I'd better keep on the alert.

"That's the front door closing," Elena says. "Do you see John outside?" she asks me.

"Yes, I do." Wearing a tee shirt, short pants, and sneakers, he's running briskly down the street.

"I had better go to the attic," says the High Priest, getting up. When he sees I'm not moving, he asks, "Leo . . . , I mean Wrappa-Hamen, are you not going to help me?"

Humph, the nerve! Did he side with me against Elena last night? Did he say to her that making me sleep in the hallway on a pillow was vile?

No! The pusillanimous High Priest kept quiet and got a good night's sleep in a nice bedroom in a comfortable bed while I slept in the hall on a pillow. Let him carry his own bags. Besides, I've better things to do than schlep luggage around. Snooping, for instance.

I go over to the door and wait for him to open it. Of course I could do it myself, but I can make a quicker exit if he does it for me. When the door opens, I get down on all fours and run out into the hall, tail on high. I hide behind a half column holding the bronze bust of a mustached fellow.

"Where are you, you lazy old cat?" the High Priest calls.

His footsteps are getting closer. He stops by the column. I make myself as small as possible, and after wasting his breath on some more name-calling, he walks away. From my hiding place, I watch him hurry to the little door to the servants' stairs, open it, and start walking up to the attic.

Good riddance!

There are doors to my left and my right, and I intend to find out what's behind them. I get up on my hind legs, leave my hiding place, go over to the door closest to me, and push the handle down. When the door doesn't open, I push harder. It's locked. I try the next door. Much to my surprise and displeasure, this one is also locked . . .

Two minutes later, I'm quite angry. I've tried all the doors on the floor, except for the door to Elena and the High Priest's bedroom of course, only to discover they're all locked.

What kind of home is it that locks its doors against snoopers, I mean, guests?

I feel I'm being watched. Maybe it's what the humans call a guilty conscience, or maybe it's just all these portraits lining the walls.

One is of a woman in a garden. She's beautiful. Her pose is relaxed. She wears her hair loose—it's dark and wavy like the wig of an ancient Egyptian woman. A silk ribbon encircles her head. Her dress is low-cut, and a thin ribbon gathers the folds under her breasts. The material is a light blue silk that shines like silver and looks as smooth as ice.

One of the woman's hands rests on an urn sitting on a marble pedestal. The other is beside her thigh and holds a fan of feathers. The bottom of the frame has a name written on it. Gainsborough.

I study the other portraits, but my thoughts go back to the Gainsborough. Something is troubling me about that painting, but I can't quite put my paw on it—

I hear heavy footsteps. It must be the High Priest with the luggage. I scurry back to my hiding place behind the column. He has a piece of luggage in each hand, and my carrier bag is hanging from his neck. As soon as he passes me and goes into the bedroom, I descend the grand staircase to the ground floor.

The main hallway is covered by big black and white tiles waxed to a mirror finish. I pass a huge fireplace. A fire has been lit, and the waves of warmth are comforting. When I come to a door that's ajar, I give it a push and enter.

I'm in a library, and when the High Priest sees it, he'll be green with envy. Shelves filled with books, most of them leather-bound, go up to the ceiling. It's the biggest library I've ever seen, surpassing his papyrus collection in ancient Egypt and Elena's library in New York. Heavy curtains cover the windows, and the darkness, along with the silence, makes me feel as if I were in a temple.

I'm thinking that this is a good place to meditate on what's been troubling me about the portrait upstairs when someone gets up from the high-backed leather chair I'm standing behind.

I almost be-piss myself.

"You lazy cat," a figure says, keeping its back to me. "I have been wondering how long it would take you to get down here."

I come even closer to be-pissing myself, but as I'm about to lose control of my bladder, I recognize the voice. It's the High Priest!

"How, how, did you get down here before I did?"

"Calm yourself," he says, turning around. "I took the secret passage."

"What secret passage?"

"If I told you, it would no longer be a secret."

I'm bursting with curiosity. "I promise I won't tell anybody."

"Umm. If I remember correctly, no one helped me carry the luggage from the attic to the bedroom."

"I was just thinking of your health," I say, trying my best to sound sincere. "You have a bit of a stomach. I thought some exercise would do you good."

He clears his throat and asks, "Is it very noticeable?"

"No, no. Only to a keen eye like mine."

"Elena has a keen eye. Do you think she has noticed it?" His voice is trembling.

"Not that I know of. But I'm sure Elena would love you anyway."

Is that a bead of sweat I see on his forehead?

72

"Wrappa-Hamen, you must tell me the truth. Did Elena say I was getting fat?"

"If I remember correctly, you said there's a secret passage in the house . . ."

"You win. It is behind the mirrored wall in the bedroom."

"How did you find it?"

The High Priest doesn't answer.

"Okay. Elena has never mentioned your stomach to me."

He breathes a sigh of relief. "It was pure chance," he explains. "In the middle of the night I suddenly woke up. I saw a pale light coming from underneath the mirrored wall and heard faint footsteps behind it."

"Were you scared?"

"Just curious. I got out of bed, careful not to wake Elena, and looked for a hidden door in the wall. I found a small lever behind a curtain. When I turned it, a narrow door opened."

"Was anyone there?"

"No. And there was complete darkness. John had shown us a box of candles and matches he left on top of the dresser in case of a power failure. I lit a candle and went through the door to a small landing with a locked door and a descending stairway that led me to a wall. When I touched it, it gave way, and I found myself here in the library."

"Where in the library exactly?"

"Over there," he says, pointing to a large marble fireplace. "I had to crouch a little to get through. Then the wall closed behind me. When I pushed it, it opened again."

"Why didn't you say something this morning to Elena and me?"

"I did not want her to know I had spent the night in the library reading. You know how she feels about everyone getting enough sleep."

"But what about me?"

"You gave me no chance. I was going to tell you when we left to get the luggage, but you disappeared into thin air."

I can't argue with that!

"When you got back to the bedroom with the luggage, didn't Elena see you disappear behind the wall?"

"No, she was bathing Alexander. If she had seen me, she would have followed me, even if it meant taking Alexander with her."

He's right. Elena's as big a snoop as he is—or as I am.

"So, what were you reading that kept you here all night?"

"Most of these books deal with ancient Egyptian history. I read some of them."

"Why would you want to read about ancient Egypt? We come from there."

"There are many things I do not know about our history. Besides, I like to read theories modern man has about us. Some of them are quite amusing."

"The lady of the house wrote to Elena that she was interested in Egyptology and had lived in Egypt. When she comes back, you can have conversations with her."

"Umm . . . I cannot quite put my finger on it, but something is not what it seems to be."

"I know how you feel. Have you looked at the portraits in the hall upstairs?"

"Only briefly, when I went to get the luggage and when I came back carrying it."

Is he ever going to stop reminding me of my disappearing act? "Well, there's something about one that bothers me—"

I hear the front door open and close, then heavy breathing.

"I think John has returned," I say, immediately getting down on all fours.

When he reaches the open door of the library, he stops to look inside. He's red in the face and sweating. "Mr. Knowall, I trust you like madam's library."

"I find it quite interesting."

I go over to John and rub against his bare hairy legs. It doesn't bother me that they're wet. He bends down and pets me on the back. His hand is warm.

"Is there anything I can do for you, sir?"

"No, John. We are, I mean, I am fine."

"Then I'll go and take my shower." He bows his head slightly before leaving.

"A nice fellow," I remark. "And someone who takes good care

of his body. Not a trace of a protruding stomach on him."

"We should get back to Elena," the High Priest says curtly. "She must be wondering what has happened to us. You had better stay down on your fours."

"Why? Who's going to see me in the secret passage?"

"First, we are not going up that way. We are taking the main staircase. Second, John might make use of the secret passage. I do not know who was in there last night before I discovered the lever that opened the door. And third, Elena would learn of its existence when she saw us come through the hidden door, and I still do not want her to know about it."

"Why not?"

"If I want to read at night, I can do so without her giving me a sermon about it."

We go out into the hall, up the main staircase, and into the bedroom.

"Where did you get to?" Elena asks us.

She doesn't give us a chance to make up a lie, so we say nothing.

"And where is John? He promised me he'd take care of Alexander while we were out."

As if on cue, there's a knock on the door. Elena says, "Come in," and John appears. He cuts quite a figure dressed in a white shirt, thin black tie, long-tailed black jacket, gray vest and pants.

"Oh, there you are, John," Elena says, looking embarrassed. "We'll be going then."

John scoops up the little Pharaoh and sets him on his shoulder . . .

The Pharaoh would scoop me up and plant me on his shoulders so the crowds of people gathered to pay him honor would see me too. At such moments, I felt I was in heaven . . .

"Heeee," Alexander is crying in delight,

"Put Leopold in his carrier bag, Jack," Elena tells the High Priest, who takes me by the scruff of the neck and drops me in the bag.

That might be how one handles a normal cat, and I know the High Priest is treating me like one for John's benefit, but I don't like it!

75

"If madam doesn't require me," John says, "I'll take my leave."

"Sorry, John. Of course you may go." Elena raises a hand to the little Pharaoh's cheek. "You be a good little boy while mommy and daddy are gone."

"Mama, Dada, gud boi."

John leaves, closing the door behind him. I hear the muffled sound of the Pharaoh saying, "Gud boi, gud boi."

"I don't like being taken by the scruff of the neck!" I tell the High Priest.

"I had no choice with John here!" he replies.

"You enjoyed it."

"Now, now," Elena says, "you're acting like children. Stop it!"

"He started it," I say.

Elena puts her coat on and hands the High Priest his. He takes it with a grunt and walks to the door.

"Aren't you forgetting something?" she asks.

"I did not forget him," he says through clenched teeth. "I meant to leave him behind."

But he walks back, bends over my carrier bag, and zips it closed. Through the mesh, we exchange dirty looks. Then he picks the bag up and puts the strap over his shoulder.

"Hey, not so rough," I complain.

"Are we ready?" Elena asks impatiently.

"Yes," we growl in unison.

She sighs in relief.

Chapter 12

The High Priest and I follow Elena across across the road. She turns us around so we can admire a semi-circular terrace of five-story buildings. "This is the Royal Crescent."

In front of each building is an open space with an iron railing. Last night I saw the railing in front our our building from the opposite side when I looked out the window in the basement kitchen.

"Like the rest of the city of Bath, the Royal Crescent was built of Oolitic Limestone."

The color of the stone reminds me of honey. Dark honey in the shade, but golden in the light . . .

How happy I felt at sunrise when the limestone of ancient Egypt glowed with the renewed light, how peaceful I felt at sunset when it was set on fire, and how sad I felt when night covered it in shrouds . . .

Elena's raised voice brings me back to reality. She's giving us more details about the history of the Royal Crescent. Pretty boring stuff, but I decide to pay attention in case I'm tested.

It's too late! I get only Elena's last words. ". . . facade of Ionic columns." If she tested me right now, I'd be in a lot of trouble.

"So, Gato-Hamen, how many years did it take to build the Crescent?"

What a relief she isn't asking me!

"I know the answer, but perhaps Wrappa-Hamen would like to show you he does too."

Of all the dirty tricks!

"All right," says Elena, bending over the carrier bag to look at me. "How many years, Wrappa-Hamen?"

A few seconds pass. "Eight years," I answer. "It was begun in 1767 and completed in 1775."

"Oh, Wrappa-Hamen," Elena says, delighted. "You were listening, my darling Puss in Boat."

She straightens up and looks at the High Priest. "I bet you didn't know the answer. That's why you wanted me to ask Wrappa-Hamen!"

My carrier bag is resting on his hip, and through the thin nylon mesh, I feel him stiffen. He's asking himself how I came up with the answer. He'll never guess that when Elena bent over the carrier bag to put her question to me, I looked up and read the information on the back of the tourist map in her hand!

"Good morning, madam," I hear when we resume walking.

"Good morning, Harry," Elena replies.

Dressed in a uniform, Harry is standing in front of one of the buildings on the Royal Crescent.

"Who is he?" asks the High Priest when the man is out of earshot.

"He's the concierge of the Royal Crescent Hotel."

"But how does he know you?"

"I told you our hostess left me a pass giving me access to the hotel spa. I made good use of it while you were still in New York, remember?"

"Vaguely," he answers, annoyed he can't remember.

"If you like, later we can go for a swim. Would you enjoy that?"

"Yes, I would," he says, cheering up.

"What about me?" I ask.

"You can't go swimming with us, Wrappa-Hamen, but there's something else for you. The hotel has a front section and a back section—small buildings with more bedrooms, a restaurant, and the pool. In between is a lovely garden. You can amuse yourself there."

We walk down a street to a circle of buildings like those on the Royal Crescent. It's as if three smaller crescents had been joined together, with only a narrow road dividing one from the other. In the middle of the circle, surrounded by a wider road, is a lawn with a large shady tree in the center . . .

Stonehenge had circles of stone that stood on a green field . . .

"This is the Circus," Elena tells us. "It was designed by John Wood, but soon after building began he died. His son completed it. Gato-Hamen, do you remember his name? I'll give you a hint. He also designed the Royal Crescent."

"It is on the tip of my tongue," he says, stalling for time.

Ten seconds go by. "Well?" she asks impatiently.

I crane my neck to find the answer on the back of her map.

"John Wood the Younger."

Elena unzips the carrier bag just enough so she can pat me on the head. "My darling Puss in Boat, you are the best. Unlike this dunce," she says, pointing her thumb at the High Priest.

Again I feel him stiffen.

A man dressed in a raincoat comes out of one of the buildings on the Circus and walks in our direction. In one hand he carries a small suitcase, in the other an umbrella. He uses the umbrella like a walking stick. As he passes us, he gives us a look that can only be translated as "tourist pests."

"That man came out of number seventeen!" says Elena when he's walked on. "A very famous eighteenth-century painter lived there. Thomas Gainsborough. Our hostess owns a painting of his. A portrait of a lady in a blue dress. Has either of you noticed it?"

"I saw it this morning," I say, excited. "That reminds me. Why are the other rooms on our floor locked?"

Elena sighs. "It's not just on the first floor but the second as well. And I would like to know why myself."

"Why don't you ask John?"

No answer.

"Ah, you don't want to admit you've been snooping!"

"Well, yes. I mean, no. What I mean is, I wouldn't call it 'snooping.'"

"Elena, remember who you're talking to."

"All right. I was snooping."

"Now that's settled, there's something about the portrait of the lady in the blue dress that bothers me. But I can't quite put my paw on it."

"I also felt there was something not quite right about the portrait. But I have a degree in fine art. You knew it intuitively! I'm very impressed!"

"Have you figured out what's wrong?"

"Yes. The woman's face was later altered by someone other than Gainsborough."

"Who cares who painted the face?" the High Priest suddenly says. "We are supposed to be going to a flea market!"

He's surly because he didn't know the answers to Elena's questions and didn't notice there was something wrong with the portrait. But hearing it from me would only upset him more.

"Look at the time!" Elena says. "We should have been at the flea market by now."

She quickens her pace. The High Priest struggles to keep up with her, and I'm bounced from one side of my carrier bag to another.

We leave the Circus by one of the three streets that intersect the road around the lawn.

"The Assembly Rooms," says Elena, nodding toward a building we're rushing past. "The Costume Museum is there. We'll have to come back to visit it."

We turn right, hurry down another street, then dash across a road and almost get killed by a lorry. I'll have to remember the driver's colorful curses!

When we reach the safety of the pavement on the other side, Elena and the High Priest pause to give themselves a chance to stop shaking. I'm in shock myself.

"Have you ever heard of crossing at a traffic light?" I ask Elena when I've recovered slightly.

"Sorry," she says, still breathless.

At a slower pace, we walk to a crossing with a traffic light and turn left on a narrow piece of pavement lying between two roads. On either side of us, cars and lorries are speeding noisily by. A sign says the road we have to cross now is the Roman Road.

My nerves may be nearly shattered, but my curiosity is still intact. "Is the Roman Road named after the same Romans who conquered Egypt?" I ask Elena.

"Yes! The Romans were the first to build a city here. They named it Aquae Sulis after the goddess of healing and the natural hot springs. My parents took me to the Roman museum near Bath Abbey. The Roman baths and the remains of the temple of the Goddess Sulis are about twenty feet below street level. My father said a third-century Roman writer named Solinus had called the temple and the baths one of the wonders of the world . . . I can't wait to see them again."

The traffic light turns green, and we cross the road.

"Here it is," Elena says. "The Paragon flea market!"

We're standing before a wide shop window. Inside, it's

crowded with people walking among stalls crammed with items on display.

Through a door on the left we enter a small vestibule with a sign on the wall that says "More Antiques on the Floor Below." A doorway on the right leads us to the first stall. There's a table laden with purses, gloves, necklaces, bracelets, and other similar items.

Elena looks like a child trying to decide which sweet to choose! She picks up an oval-shaped purse made of tiny glass beads and dangles it in front of the High Priest. "Do you like it?"

"Very pretty," he says.

She pushes a small button on top and the purse opens. "I love the plastic frame."

It's the color of ivory and in the shape of two oriental sea monsters whose heads come together to form the tip of the clasp. A few strokes of blue paint are still visible.

"You have good taste," says an elderly lady at the other side of the table.

"Oh, I was just browsing." Elena puts the purse back on the table.

The lady picks it up and looks at it as if studying it. "Sixty-five pounds. That's the best I can do."

"That's all?" the High Priest comments.

"What he means is, that's too much," Elena says hastily.

The lady thinks for a few seconds. "Sixty. That's the best I can do."

The haggling reminds me of the markets in ancient Egypt. Elena takes the purse from the lady, turns it in her hand, looking at it carefully, then puts it back on the table. "Still too much."

"It's from 1920's. It's in very good condition," the lady insists. "I can't sell it for less than sixty." Elena starts to move away. "All right! I see how much you like it. You can have it for fifty-five pounds."

"It's a deal."

If Elena had lived in ancient Egypt, she would've been the bane of the merchants.

The lady wraps the purse in tissue paper, Elena pays her, and we move on. "Remember," she tells the High Priest. "When a dealer gives you a price, you always say, 'It's too much.' Got that?"

"Yes," he says, embarrassed at being scolded for his inability to bargain.

The next stall has nothing of interest for Elena. But when we reach the one after that, she gasps. "Look at that umbrella! It's from the 1930's!"

It has green, brown, and dark red stripes. The handle is as clear as glass, shaped like the handle of a sword, with traces of green paint visible in the grooves.

"Now remember what I told you," she says to the High Priest.

The dealer is a middle-aged man with a jolly face. "Is there something you'd like to see?" he asks her.

"That umbrella, over there," she says, pointing to it.

"You've a good eye. It's a lady's umbrella from the thirties with a nice lucite handle." He picks it up and passes it to her. I wonder if he notices her hand trembling as she takes it. "Go ahead. Open it."

"It's bad luck to open an umbrella indoors, but . . ." Elena points the umbrella down and opens it a tiny bit. "The rays seem all right, and there are no holes."

"It's in very good condition," the dealer points out. "Very good condition."

"How much?"

"Thirty-five pounds"

"Too much," the High Priest says.

"Thirty. That's the best I can do."

"Still too much."

"I'll take it!" says a lady standing behind us.

"What?!!" yells Elena, clutching the umbrella and turning to face the enemy.

"Your husband doesn't want to buy it for you," the lady explains, "so I'm buying it."

"No, you're not!" Elena turns back to the dealer. "I'll give you thirty-five pounds!"

"It's a deal."

On second thought, Elena might not have fared well shopping in ancient Egypt.

She pays for the umbrella, and, as soon as we leave the stall, hits the High Priest on the head with it.

"What the . . . ?!"

"Because of your cheapness, I almost lost the umbrella."

"But, but, you told me to bargain."

"You have to know when to stop."

I'm not the only one who remembers the lorry driver's curses. The High Priest repeats them, if only in a whisper.

What does Elena have in her little hands now? It's a long white scarf with fringes.

"You've a good eye," the dealer tells her. "It's a man's scarf from the twenties." He rolls the material between his fingers. "Feel this heavy silk. They don't make scarves like this any more."

"How much?" Elena asks, giving the High Priest a look that says, "Don't say a word."

"Thirty quid."

"I'll take it."

"I'll give you a bag for it," the dealer says when Elena pays.

"Thank you, but I don't need one."

"Cheers, then."

"Cheers."

"How come you did not bargain?" asks the High Priest as we move away from the stall.

"It's a gift," Elena says disdainfully. "One doesn't bargain for gifts,"

"A gift? For whom?"

"For you, of course." Elena wraps the scarf around his neck and kisses him on the cheek.

We go down to the lower floor, where she buys a few other items and the High Priest makes a purchase of his own—a small copy of Queen Nefertiti's famous bust for five quid.

I've seen pictures of the painted life-size bust in Elena's books and magazines on ancient Egypt. The beautiful Nefertiti wears a wide collar necklace of colored beads and a tall blue flat-topped headdress circled by a colored band. Long colorful streamers hang from the bottom of the headdress down her back. The gold cobra that would have flared above her brow has broken off. She smiles enigmatically—Elena calls it a Mona Lisa smile. And her left eye is missing . . .

83

Thousands of years ago the Pharaoh and I were traveling on the Nile to Menfi when we passed the ruins of a city. He told me it'd been built by Nefertiti and her husband, pharaoh Akhenaten, and dedicated to the god Aten. They named it Akhetaten. Believing Aten to be the one true God, they closed the temples of the state god Amun-Ra and the other Egyptian gods. But a few years after their deaths, the temples were reopened and the city dedicated to Aten was demolished . . .

"I'm hungry," Elena says.

"I am hungry too," the High Priest says. It's about time someone mentioned food!

We go back upstairs and leave the flea market the way we came in. The weather has changed. It's overcast now.

"John recommended a little restaurant called No. 5," Elena says. "It's at the other end of the bridge."

"It looks as if you will make use of your old umbrella," the High Priest says.

"I hope so!"

I wait until we have a bit of privacy before speaking. "That umbrella isn't big enough to cover all of us."

"Don't be pessimistic!"

It begins to rain lightly, and Elena opens her umbrella.

I smell mildew.

"When was this umbrella last used?" she asks. "I imagine the lady who owned is dead and she had it all her life."

"It is quite possible the lady had to sell her umbrella to make ends meet," the High Priest says.

"I like my story better . . . If her spirit can see me, she knows I love it."

It's raining harder.

"And if her spirit can see me," I add, "she knows my carrier bag is getting wet!"

Chapter 13

We arrive at the bridge. It has stores and restaurants on both sides. "It's a copy of a medieval bridge in Florence," Elena says, "which always had shops along its sides."

Quite a few people are crossing the bridge, mostly couples, but also some families. A father is taking a picture of his brood while his wife tries to hold a large umbrella over them and to keep them from moving, failing at both tasks. "Hurry up and take the bloody picture!" she yells at her husband.

"The restaurant is over there," Elena says. Maybe it's the police car parked by the side of the road, or the memory of almost getting killed by a lorry, which makes her say, "Let's cross at the light."

The restaurant is just off the bridge and has two large windows with displays of plants. "Good afternoon. Two?" a jolly-looking waiter says when we enter.

"Two," Elena says, closing her umbrella and putting it in a stand with other wet umbrellas.

"Is that a cat?" the man inquires, pointing at me in the carrier bag and no longer looking jolly.

"Yes," replies the High Priest.

"I'm sorry, but we can't allow animals in the restaurant."

"We were so looking forward to eating here," says Elena, in the most obsequious tone of voice I've ever heard her use.

The waiter scratches his head. "I have it," he says, jolly once again. "Leave him just outside the door."

"A splendid idea!" Elena and the High Priest reply in unison.

Traitors! I can't believe it!

"I'll give you a table near the door," the waiter adds. "You can keep an eye on your pet." He takes the carrier bag from the High Priest, opens the door, and puts me outside. He leaves the door open a few inches, and I see him seating the traitors at a nearby table.

I also see a pink-faced man eating alone at a table next to theirs. He suspends a fork laden with pasta in mid-air to study the new arrivals. Satisfied, he continues eating, stopping only to finish the last drop of wine in his glass and then order another.

85

The two traitors look over the menu and discuss it. Their table is near enough to the door for me to hear them.

"The starters all sound so scrumptious." Elena says. "I think I'll try the baby squid salad. And you?"

"I'm torn between the avocado salad vinaigrette and the fried sardines."

I'm torn as well, between two courses of action. Getting out of the carrier bag, shredding Elena's umbrella, and tightening the scarf around the High Priest's neck. Or staying put, waiting, and getting my revenge when they least expect it.

The waiter returns and Elena orders for both of them. "I'll have the baby squid salad for my starter and roast duck for my entrée. My husband will have the fried sardines and the pan-fried skate."

My stomach rumbles. I look at pink-faced man. Now he's eating a slice of chocolate cake. My stomach rumbles again. I turn my back on the traitors. Watching them stuff their faces will be too painful to bear.

It's raining harder. Drops bounce off the pavement and come through the mesh of the the carrier bag. Soon I'm not just hungry but also wet.

"Hello, puss." The pink-faced man is bending over the carrier bag and looking at me through the mesh. "How many stars would you give this restaurant?" he asks teasingly.

I smell all his indulgences on his breath and look him straight in the eye. "Four," I say, loud and clear.

His pink face turns read. He straightens up and shakes his head in disbelief. "I shouldn't have had so much to drink. I must be pissed."

I meow. He gives a sigh of relief and walks away.

"Maybe five," I say when he's gone a few steps. He quickens his pace, then breaks into a run. It'll be a while before he teases a poor starving cat again!

"Wrappa-Hamen," I hear in a whisper. It's Elena. She's bending over me with a small plate in her hand. The High Priest is with her. He unzips my carrier bag, and she places the dish inside.

"Well," he says. "We'll leave you to it then." They go back inside the restaurant.

On the plate is a fried sardine, some baby squid, a piece of skate, and a slice of roast duck. I take a bite of the sardine, and move the morsel around in my mouth, spitting out the bones as I find them. When it's safe, I swallow, thin crusty skin and all.

Remembering what I thought of doing to Elena's brolly and the High Priest's neck makes me feel guilty. Then I start eating the baby squid and, mercifully, forget everything else.

When the plate is empty, I look into the restaurant to see how my good friends are doing. Dessert is on the table, a slice of chocolate cake for Elena, and a small terrine, which I suspect contains crème brûlée, for the High Priest. She's devouring her dessert, but he's ignoring his, admiring the little bust of Nefertiti instead of eating.

"Really, Gato-Hamen," Elena says. "Why would an ancient Egyptian want a copy of an Egyptian artifact? And a copy in such poor condition. Really." She takes a sip of coffee.

"Copy?" he says. "This is the real thing. A smaller version of the big bust."

"Whaaat. . . ?!" She sprays him with coffee. "Are you sure?" she asks, after a little coughing.

The High Priest blots his face. "Of course I am!"

"But why is another original bust missing the same eye?"

"I do not know."

"You realize it's priceless?"

It's Elena who could learn how to shop at a flea market from the High Priest, not the other way around!

"I just thought it was nice."

"You'd better put it away. You won't want anyone to know what you have."

He calmly rewraps the bust and puts it back in his pocket, then takes a spoon and digs into his crème brûlée. I hear the sugar crust crackle on impact.

But I wouldn't want any even if it were offered. I can't take my mind off the High Priest's bust of Nefertiti.

"We're going home with the bust," Elena says when he finishes his dessert and is licking his spoon. "It's too dangerous to walk around with it. It might be stolen. You might lose it or break it."

"I will be careful."

"We're going back."

She signals the waiter for the bill, and while she pays, the High Priest comes out to collect the empty plate.

"I've overheard everything," I say.

He smiles. "Do you think I should tell Elena the bust is a fake?"

"What?! Why did you tell her it was real in the first place?"

"I did not want her to think she was the only one who knew how to buy."

The High Priest has brass balls. Too bad he'll lose them when Elena finds out he's lied to her.

I'm about to give him my sympathy when she comes out of the restaurant followed by the waiter. "I like cats," he says, taking the plate from the High Priest. "I even have one myself. I hope he won't hold a grudge."

I won't!

Chapter 14

When we return to our building on the Royal Crescent, Elena looks for her keys and, realizing she's forgotten to take them, rings the bell. A few minutes go by before a panting red-faced John opens the door, cookie crumbs on the front of his jacket. The little Pharaoh is tucked under his right arm, his face smeared with chocolate pudding. John holds the door open for us.

"Mama," the little Pharaoh says, holding his arms out towards Elena.

John sets him down on the hallway floor, and she scoops him up. "I hope Alexander wasn't too much trouble."

"No, madam. He's been a perfect joy."

John is still panting from whatever game they've been playing. The little Pharaoh might not have been pulling his tail, but I'm certain the poor man has been put through some form of torture.

"Did you miss Mommy and Daddy?" Elena asks the little Pharaoh.

The High Priest takes out a handkerchief and tries to clean the Pharaoh's mouth, but he keeps turning away.

A perfect joy, indeed!

"Has madam and sir been to the Roman Museum?"

"No, John. But it's our next stop. We've come home to drop off our flea market purchases, and Leopold."

I wasn't told about this!

"I see."

The High Priest puts my carrier bag on the floor and lifts me out. I look at him inquisitively, and he shrugs his shoulders.

"We'll freshen up and then be off to the museum," Elena says. "Would you mind taking care of Alexander again, John? He'd so enjoy playing in the park."

John sighs. "It'll be a pleasure, madam."

"Thank you, John."

We leave him and go upstairs. I'm eager to get to the bedroom so I can complain to Elena. "Why do I have to stay home?" I ask once the door is closed.

"Oh, Puss in Boat, you won't be allowed in the museum. And

Gato-Hamen can't hide you under his coat again. Remember what happened at the Metropolitan Museum in New York?"

When I remain quiet, she answers for me. "No? Well, let me refresh your memory. You were discovered by the guards under his coat. Both of you were chased out of the museum, got lost, almost froze to death in the snow. And . . . should I continue?"

"No, please," I say, embarrassed. "I've heard enough,"

"Then it's settled. And you, Gato-Hamen. Put the bust of Nefertiti in a safe place."

He takes it out of his pocket and sets it on the mantle piece. Elena looks at it in awe. "I still can't believe it." If only she knew she was right to be incredulous!

After she and the High Priest have freshened up—a human euphemism for using the toilet—she lays the little Pharaoh in his crib. "I'll tell John to let Alexander nap awhile before taking him out."

I'm sure John will welcome the break!

I crawl by the little Pharaoh's side. Elena kisses him on the head, then kisses me. Whatever rancor may have been left is dissipated by her loving kiss. The High Priest also kisses his son. I give him a look that tells him he shouldn't even think about kissing me too.

By the time Elena and the High Priest close the door behind them, the little Pharaoh is sleeping, and not long after, while listening to his peaceful breathing, I too fall asleep. Mercifully, I don't dream about any ghosts . . .

John's struggling wakes me up. Poor man! He's trying to put a coat on the little Pharaoh, who wants nothing to do with it and is twisting and turning, intent not to let him win. I'm too drowsy to move.

"Shush," John says to the little Pharaoh, who's laughing heartily. "Be a good boy. You don't want to wake up Leopold."

Somehow he manages to get the coat on. He picks the little Pharaoh up and walks toward the door. When he reaches the fireplace, he stops to take a close look at the bust of Nefertiti on the mantel. "Amazing!"

What does he mean? Forgetting for a second I'm supposed to be a normal cat, I almost ask him.

After staring at the bust a while longer, he tip-toes out of the bedroom with the little Pharaoh in his arms.

Left alone, I push a chair over to the fireplace, climb up on it, and stand on my hind legs to examine the bust. It's beautiful, but I don't think John was referring to its beauty.

I take it in my forepaws to study it more closely, but the sudden sound of a car alarm startles me, and it slips from my grasp. I watch helplessly as it crashes on the floor and disintegrates.

Elena will kill me! But wait. The High Priest will tell her the bust was a worthless. She might even have a good laugh.

Convinced I have nothing to worry about, I get down from the chair and push it back to the table by the window, where I catch sight of John pushing the little Pharaoh across the road in a stroller.

I look around the room for something to scoop up the bits of plaster, don't find anything suitable, and decide to just cover them. I search through a dresser for a scarf or kerchief, but find instead a package of the little Pharaoh's nappies. I take one out, spread it open, and cover the debris.

My efforts have made me hungry, and I see myself making a peanut butter sandwich in the basement kitchen.

That's exactly what I'm doing when I hear what sounds like a door or window slamming repeatedly. I stop and listen. The noise is coming from the ground floor. I have to investigate. I quickly finish making my sandwich, eat it on the spot, then go upstairs to the main hall.

The noise is coming from a room at the back of the building, a room I haven't seen yet. I walk over to the door, gently push it open, and see a long dining table lined with chairs. The curtains are drawn, but moving. Slipping behind them, I see the French door has been left open and the wind is banging the two panels together.

If only all mysteries were so easily solved!

I go through the French door into a garden and follow a narrow path of white pebbles to a fountain with a large basin. White and pink water lilies float on the water. In the middle of the basin is a column supporting a smaller basin. Water from its spout trickles down into the large basin, and as the water moves, so do the water lilies.

Sounds of laughter and the clanking of dishes are coming from behind the garden wall to the right. Bushes of roses grow by the wall, which is covered in ivy. I tread carefully through the rose bushes to avoid getting pricked by the thorns. When I get to the wall, I use the ivy as a ladder. From the top of the wall, I see, a few gardens down, a small group of people having tea under large striped umbrellas.

It must be the garden of the Royal Crescent Hotel, which we passed this morning.

Going from one garden wall to another, I reach the hotel garden. I consider mingling with the people having tea until I discover, much to my horror, that there are little children playing on the grass. Given what the little Pharaoh does to my tail, I hate to imagine what a whole group of children might do to it!

I stay on the wall, and moving behind the branch of a tree so I won't be seen, I watch and listen.

"I feel like a new woman," says a woman in a red jacket to a woman in a dress with a floral print.

"How's that?"

"I used the swimming pool and had a massage as well. You should try it."

"I don't want to be seen in a swimsuit until I finish my diet." She butters a scone, then covers it with a small mountain of jam.

"When did you start dieting?" asks the woman in the red jacket says.

"I haven't," the other woman replies, taking a large bite of her scone.

At another table, a fancily dressed older lady laden with jewelry is sipping tea with a man young enough to be her son. He leans forward in his chair and takes her hand, the one with a large sapphire ring. "You grow more beautiful each day."

"Charles, you are such a liar, but at my age, being lied to is better than being ignored."

"But I mean it."

"You're such a dear boy," she says. She takes her hand away, looks in her purse, takes out a thin box wrapped in gold paper and red ribbon, and presents it to him.

Almost in a frenzy, he grabs the box from her hand, pulls at the ribbon, and tears at the paper. He opens the white box inside, takes out a wallet made of crocodile skin, then frowns in disappointment.

"Open it," the lady says.

Charles looks in the wallet. I can't see what's inside, but judging from the big smile on his face, it's stuffed with money.

He gets up from his chair, stands behind the lady, then leans down and kisses her on the back of the neck. When she turns her head, he kisses her on the mouth. When they finish kissing he helps her up, and hand in hand they disappear into one of the buildings at the rear of the garden. A maid arrives and hastily clears away their unfinished tea.

I'm trying to figure out how to get down the wall and into the garden without the children spotting me when a cumulus begins to unload its heavy cargo.

A lot of scurrying ensues. Guests abandon their tea and run for shelter. Parents scoop up their children and carry them off. The woman in the red jacket pulls it up over her head and flees. The woman in the floral-print dress is right behind her, holding a shopping bag over her head with one hand and clutching a scone with the other. Within seconds, everyone has disappeared.

A large wooden door slowly opens in the building behind the secluded area of the garden to reveal a man in a dripping-wet swimsuit and the famous hotel pool. The man looks outside for a while, then turns around, and, descending a few steps, goes back into the pool and disappears.

The wall I'm on connects with the wall beside the secluded area of the garden. When the rain lets up, I walk straight to it, then along it, and jump down near the open door. Staying close to the ground, I peep inside.

The pool looks like the Roman pool in Elena's guide book. The man I saw is the only one in the water. He's floating on his back. On the other side of the pool are lounge chairs, two large barrels filled with water, and two doors. One door says steam room, the other sauna. Beside each door there's an open shower.

A girl in white uniform comes in through a doorway on the side, walks to the far end of the pool, and lights a large candle on the floor. She puts something in a dish near the candle, then leaves the way she came in. Smoke begins to rise from the dish.

It's incense, myrrh. This place is like a temple!

A woman in a swimsuit comes out of the steam room, little puffs of steam following her. She turns the shower on, but instead of getting under the water, she gathers it in her cupped hands and splashes her face. Then she walks to the edge of the pool, waves at the man, who waves back, and lies down on a lounge chair.

The man turns on his stomach and swims frog style to the end of the pool, stopping under a large faucet and pushing a button. Water comes out in a strong jet. He puts his shoulders under it and moans with pleasure. When the water stops, he swims back, climbs out, and stands beside the woman. "Rose, did the steam room help?"

"Yes! So relaxing. I feel like a new woman."

"Good. What we need now is a nice cocktail."

"Splendid idea."

He helps Rose up and hand in hand they disappear through doorway the girl in white used.

Steam room! So relaxing! I have to try it. I've been feeling tense ever since Stonehenge.

I go through the door, down the steps, and over to the pool. I jump in, quickly swim across, climb out, and go to the steam room. I get up on my hind legs and pull on the door handle with all my might. The door opens just enough for me to get inside.

The warm fog is so thick I can't see. I go down on my fours, take a few steps forward, and bump into something wet, bony, and bristly.

A human shin?

A woman's loud scream confirms it is.

I back away, then turn around, searching for the door. The woman has the same idea. I feel her lower leg brush against my side.

Another loud scream.

Blinded by the steam, I can't see where I'm going. The woman has the same problem. Scrambling, she almost trips over me.

This scream is so loud it makes my fur stand on end.

Suddenly, I feel cold air as the door opens in front of me. As I run out, I see the girl in white holding it. Not stopping to rinse my face, I fly into the pool, race across, jump out, leap up the steps and out the door. I climb up the garden wall, run till I reach my garden, then jump down.

Steam room! So relaxing! I'm now more tense than ever. I wonder what the sauna is like!

Luckily no one's closed the door to the dining room. I go inside and, breathless, begin to dry myself with the curtains, my ears ringing from the woman's screams.

Why is the ringing becoming louder?

It's Elena yelling at the top of her lungs!

I run out of the dining room, into the hall, and straight up the main staircase to the bedroom. The door is ajar, but I don't go in because of what I see inside. Elena's swinging a diaper about as if it were the proverbial dead cat.

"I can't believe he broke it," she screams, "and look how he tried to cover it up!" She presses the diaper under the High Priest's nose. "A priceless piece of art like that, and he broke it!" Now she's wringing the diaper. "I will kill him!"

I feel my balls shrink, and it's not from being wet and cold.

What's the High Priest waiting for? Why doesn't he tell her the truth?

"Elena," he says after what seems like an eternity, "the piece was a fake."

"What?" She plunks herself down on a chair.

"I am sorry, Elena. I just wanted to show you I could find a real bargain . . ."

"I see." I know that when she says, "I see," it actually means, "I don't see and I'm still furious."

How does one appease an angry woman? With a gift, of course.

But what sort of gift can I give Elena? I've got it. A rose.

And where am I going to get a rose? In the garden, of course.

In a flash, I'm down the stairs, through the French door, and back in the garden. I stand upright to better see what's available and spot the perfect rose, a large yellow one, which, unfortunately, is in the very middle of the rose bush. As I make my way toward it, thorns prick me, but that's a small price to pay.

I reach up to my prize, break the stem off the branch, and

carefully put it in my mouth. Then I back out of the rose bush, get down on my fours again, and head inside.

When I get upstairs, I peek in the bedroom. The mood has certainly changed. Elena and the High Priest are laughing! John is also there now, holding a broom in one hand and a dust pan in the other.

"It was foolish of me to get so upset, wasn't it, John?" Elena says.

"Not foolish at all, madam. I saw the bust on the mantle when I came in to pick up little Alexander. I know something about antiques, especially Egyptian antiques, and immediately realized the bust was as old as the larger one, the famous Nefertiti head."

John's words have a terrible effect on his listeners. Elena looks as if she's about to faint, the High Priest collapses on the bed, and I bite the rose stem so hard one of the thorns pierces my tongue.

The pain is excruciating, but I can't cry out. If Elena were to find me now, I'd certainly experience even worse. I let my beautiful rose fall from my mouth and try to think of a place to hide.

"Madam, I forgot to tell you that your hostess rang earlier," I hear John say as I begin my retreat. "She's instructed me to convey her regrets she won't be able to dine with you tonight. She's been delayed in London."

"Thank you, John," Elena replies in a stern voice. "But dinner is the last thing on my mind tonight."

I know what Elena has first on her mind. Murder, feline murder.

It's time for me to make my getaway. Remembering all the other rooms on this floor and the second floor are locked, I make my way up to the next floor, the attic, where I jump into the magic boat and collapse.

There are those who say cats have an easy life. They couldn't be more wrong!

Chapter 15

I'm cold, so I go in the cabin and cover myself with a blanket. When I no longer feel the cold, it's my stomach that begins to trouble me. It's empty and, worse, it's going to stay that way, for I dare not venture out. Elena might be lying in wait behind the kitchen door.

If I fall asleep, I won't feel the pain in my tongue, or the one in my belly, or the one in my heart. But sleep doesn't come. As any Egyptian would, I try counting donkeys. "One donkey, two donkeys, three donkeys, four donkeys, five donkeys, six donkeys, seven donkeys, eight donkeys, nine donkeys, ten . . ."

I doze off, but have nightmares. In one, my tongue is so swollen I can't eat the roast chicken placed in front of me. In another, Elena is hitting me on the head with a huge rose. In yet another, the steam room becomes a train station with a steam locomotive puffing smoke in my face, blinding and choking me—

Mercifully, a bray wakes me up. Forgetting where I am, I look for a donkey. But of course there are no donkeys here. I hear the sound again. It's not a bray, but a woman's cry.

Elena's? I have to investigate.

I get out of the boat, leave the attic, creep down to the first floor, and put my ear to the door of the bedroom. All is quiet in there but for the familiar sound of the High Priest's snores. One low snore, then a pause, two low snores in a row and another pause, three loud snores in a row with a longer pause. To make doubly sure the cry I heard wasn't Elena's I open the door and peek. She's there, sleeping soundly.

Which means she isn't lying in wait for me behind the kitchen door!

I close the door to the bedroom, go to the servants' staircase and down the corridor to the kitchen, where I make myself a peanut butter sandwich. But when I take a bite, I feel a sharp pain in my tongue. The pain is so bad I can't eat. I spit the morsel into the kitchen sink, grab a pot cover to use as a mirror, and stick my tongue out. It's red and swollen.

As I dispose of my sandwich in the bin, I sense a presence and quickly turn. A shadowy figure disappears down the corridor. I run after it. It's gone. But there's an odor. It's familiar, but I can't identify it.

I follow it up the servants' staircase to the main hall and into the library over to the fireplace. The back wall of the fireplace is open. The odor is coming from the secret passage. I enter and see the steps leading up toward the bedroom. There are also steps going down.

The High Priest forgot to mention them? Or they weren't here before?

Following the odor, I descend to a narrow landing. I must be as deep as the basement by now, but the steps continue. The way down is long. I feel as if I've descended to the bowels of the earth by the time the steps end. They've led me to a small door. I get up on my hind legs, hold my breath, and slowly turn the handle.

It's an ancient Egyptian tomb!

The ceiling and walls are painted with scenes that celebrate life, scenes of harvest, hunting, and fishing. In the middle of the ceiling is a disk representing the sun. From it stretch human arms, and from the hands come sunrays, just as in my dream. The tomb is lit by oil lamps placed on high narrow tables, each an exact replica of an ancient one. The smell of incense is overpowering, but it's not the odor that led me here.

Why is the tomb here? And where's the sarcophagus?

Curiosity and fascination overcome my fear, and I move further inside. At the far end of the hall is a bed. Each side is shaped like a leopard. On the wall behind it, painted in gold, is the same image of the sun with outstretched arms. The odor that led me here is stronger than ever.

I feel someone is watching me. I swallow hard and slowly turn.

Standing before me is woman in a hooded white woolen robe. The hood has been pulled over her head, and she hides her face with her hands. I climb onto the bed so I can reach her face and take her hands down. She's wearing a gold mask, the mask of the High Priestess of Stonehenge . . .

Of course! The odor is her smell. I should have recognized it sooner. But how can she be here?

With trembling paws, I remove the mask. I look into the face whose beauty has been revered by both the ancient world and the modern. It's the face made famous by her bust.

"Queen Nefertiti."

"Wrappa-Hamen."

"You remember my name?"

"I have kept your name here," she says, pointing to her heart, "for thousands of years."

"But it was only the other day we met in Stonehenge."

"For me, thousands of years have passed since I last saw you."

Talking has made my tongue swell again. "I'v zo many quezions fo u. I don knuw whe to begi."

"What's wrong?"

"It'z mi tung. It'z zwollen. It hutz."

"Sit down and stick your tongue out." Cupping my chin in one hand, she puts two fingers into my mouth and, with maternal care, pulls a thorn from my tongue. The pain is gone immediately. I lick her hand. She smiles and sits next to me on the bed.

"Queen Nefertiti, how can you still be alive?"

"I cannot die. I do not know why. A few years after the death of my husband, Pharaoh Akhenaten, I was murdered by assassins but awoke as if from sleep. With the help of those few I could still trust, I faked my burial and fled . . . If Egypt did not want Nefertiti, then I no longer wanted Egypt."

"At Stonehenge, why didn't you tell Gato-Hamen and me who you were?"

"I was ashamed. You told me he was the High Priest of the god Amun-Ra and the goddess Bastet was your protector. My husband, Akhenaten, and I had closed the temples of Amun-Ra and the temples of the other Egyptian gods, including those of Bastet. I was also ashamed I was still alive. Egyptians seek immortality in the world above. There, I would reign as a queen. But here, the great Nefertiti dwells in the shadows like a criminal. Because I cannot die, I am denied the splendid immortality that befits me and must endure a futile existence that debases me."

"You see immortality as a curse, but many people would see it as a blessing."

"They are fools. I am a slave to all I have witnessed over the centuries. You cannot know, Wrappa-Hamen, what it means to live with ancient memories that remain as fresh as the rose you picked for Elena in the garden."

How did she see me? From one of the locked rooms, using the secret passage?

"I have traveled all over the world. Whenever my failure to age might become noticeable, I moved and assumed a new identity. But then Borchardt's expedition unearthed my bust. When it was exhibited in the Egyptian Museum of Berlin in 1923, my face appeared in newspapers all over the world. Since then, I have lived in near seclusion, wearing large hats that hide my face."

"Why did you come to Bath?"

"I consider Bath my second home after Akhetaten. I was here when the Royal Crescent was being built. I had young Wood design this room and the secret passages. I swore him to secrecy. It was still a time when a man's word was his bond. He just assumed I was an eccentric. In this country, eccentricity is not unusual."

"To conceal your immortality, surely you had to leave Bath as well."

"Of course. Before selling this house, I had the entrances to the secret passage walled up. I missed Bath and longed to returned. When the house was again for sale, I bought it. I have lived here ever since."

"Was the Gainsborough portrait of you?" I ask, knowing the answer already. "Did you alter the face after your bust was discovered?"

"Yes. I posed for Gainsborough while he was living here in Bath. He would not accept payment. He said that being allowed to bask in my exotic beauty was more than payment enough. I had treasured his gift for a century and a half and could not bring myself to destroy it. But I had to alter the face."

Nefertiti has told me so much, but I still have a question. "Was it you who appeared to me in my dreams and in the mirror in New York?"

"Yes. It was my unbearable, indescribable pain defying time and distance."

"But why me?"

"You are the one . . ." The words sound familiar.

100

"I am the one? What does it mean?"

She takes a deep breath, then slowly lets it out.

"Just after World War II I was on the Paddington train on my way back to Bath. The only other person in my compartment was a young woman blinded by bomb shrapnel during the Blitz. She told me something she said had told no one else. Her blindness had left her with psychic powers. If she touched someone or was touched, she would see the person's future—"

"That doesn't answer my question."

"Please let me finish," Nefertiti says, raising her hand. "The conductor came into the compartment to check her ticket, and their hands touched. When he left, she was very upset. I asked her what she had seen. 'Death,' she said. 'Very soon.'"

"Like you, she'd been cursed with a gift."

"Yes. She told me she tried her best to avoid being touched, but because she was blind, she was constantly being offered an arm or a hand. She was taking the train to Bristol, where she would live with an older sister in seclusion . . ."

Nefertiti sighs deeply before continuing her story.

"I did not dare touch her, afraid she might discover my secret. The train arrived at Bath, we said goodbye, and a porter took my bags. I was walking along the platform when I realized I had taken her gloves. I ran back to the compartment, but the train had begun to move. The window was down, and I yelled to her to take the gloves. She reached for them, and our hands touched . . . Her face suddenly went pale. With her opaque eyes staring into darkness, she uttered the words that have haunted me ever since. 'Neither man nor beast will set you free, but the hybrid in between.' I immediately remembered you from Stonehenge thousands of years in the past and knew that Nanette meant you."

"The blind woman's name was Nanette? In New York City I met a blind woman named Nanette at an old people's home. When I touched her, she screamed, 'You are the one. You are the one.' I thought she was raving."

"Nanette saw into your future as she had seen into mine. You —a hybrid of man and animal—are the one who will set me free."

When the High Priest read the Tarot cards for me, he said the Fool meant that who I was would determine where my journey would take me. I'm the hybrid Nanette foresaw, and Nefertiti has brought me to Bath!

"I had to wait for the twentieth-first century to search for you," she continues. "In Stonehenge, you had told me the first name of the woman you lived with in New York City. Not much to go on. I was becoming desperate when I read an article in *Egyptian Antiquities* by Elena Knowall. She was identified as a freelance writer living in New York. Her article contained information about a certain artifact's role in the burial ceremony which only an ancient Egyptian well versed in our religious practices could possess. I thought of the High Priest and knew I had the right Elena. I wrote. She answered. You know the rest."

"Is John aware of who you are and who I am?"

"Of course. He is my loyal servant, a descendant of the priests of Stonehenge. And there is something you should know about John. His hobby is making replicas of Egyptian artifacts"—she seems to be suppressing a smile—"and he sells them to a dealer at the flea market."

The bust of Nefertiti was his. When he saw it on the mantelpiece and said "amazing," he was admiring his own work.

"But why did he tell Elena the bust was real?"

"There is something else you should know about John. He has a warped sense of humor. I laughed so much when he told me how you had covered the mess with a diaper and that he had then told Elena the bust was real. I had not laughed like that in centuries."

"You say I'm the one who will set you free. What do you mean?"

"I want to be free of my immortality. There is only one way to achieve that, and you are the only one who can do it." The look on her face tells me what she wants of me.

"Never!" I cry. "I could never kill you. No matter what Nanette predicted."

"You accursed cat," Nefertiti yells, "will you have me live forever?! In pain and anguish!"

"Killing you would be a terrible crime."

"A crime? The crime is that I have lived thousands of years beyond my life span. I had given up all hope of dying. This room was my place of rest and meditation, an ancient Egyptian world beneath Georgian Bath. But when Nanette told me you would set me free, I knew it would be my tomb."

"I won't kill you. I can't."

"You can. You must! Wrappa-Hamen, I'm tired. I wish to rest. I desire death."

"I can't kill you!"

'Yes, you can. I will show you what you must do." Nefertiti gets up, adds incense to the burner, and disappears into the shadows. The air is soon saturated with the intoxicating odor. I feel I'm about to faint.

Am I'm beginning to see things? No. It's really the High Priest coming toward the bed.

"I thought you were asleep," I say, "snoring."

"Elena does not fall asleep until she thinks I have. I was only pretending to sleep so I could go down to the library and read."

"How did you find me?"

"I took the secret passage to the library. The wall behind the fireplace was already opened, and I saw steps I had not seen before. They continued downward. As I descended, I began to smell incense. The odor led me here."

"You'll never believe—"

"I know it all. I have been listening behind the door. Just as I predicted, a high priestess has revealed her secrets to you. And to think you doubted me!"

"Have mercy. Not now." I'm no longer able to sit up.

Nefertiti emerges from the shadows. The High Priest bows so low his head almost touches the bed. "Queen Nefertiti," he says. "Never was a name more appropriate. Nefertiti—the Beautiful One Has Come."

"We meet again, Gato-Hamen. Or should I say Jack?"

"Why did you hide from us?"

"I was waiting for a chance to be alone with Wrappa-Hamen. I had to tell him he was the one destined to kill me, the only being on earth that could kill me . . . But he wants to deny his destiny."

Nefertiti bends over me, coming so close her face is all I see. I'm no longer admiring her beauty, but fearing it. "You must kill me!" she cries.

Her command sends chills up and down my spine. I try to

protest, but the words don't come. I shake my head.

Nefertiti straightens up and laughs hysterically. She has a knife in her right hand and plunges it into her chest. Blood begins to flow from the wound, staining her gown.

The last thing I see before losing consciousness is the High Priest rushing to her side.

Chapter 16

When I wake up, I feel as if I were in the middle of an earthquake. I open my eyes and look into the High Priest's face. He's holding me like a baby and carrying me up the servants' stairs. With every step he takes I receive a jolt.

"Good morning," he says.

"If you had the dream I had, you wouldn't be saying that."

"Dream?"

"I should say, nightmare."

"What was it about?"

"Queen Nefertiti wanted me to kill her, and when I wouldn't, she killed herself."

"Wrappa-Hamen, that was no dream."

"No dream? Nefertiti is dead?"

"Yes. I mean, no"

"What in the name of Bastet are you telling me?!"

I yell so loud that the High Priest is startled and begins to lose his footing. Afraid he's going to fall, I leap down from his arms. He sways back and forth, but manages to regain his balance.

I climb up a few steps, turn around—why is his head shaved? —and look down at him straight into his eyes. "Did Nefertiti really ask me to kill her? And did she kill herself?"

Maybe it's my murderous stare, but he gives me a clear answer. "Yes to the first, no to the second."

"But I saw her kill herself."

"Remember, Wrappa-Hamen. Nefertiti is cursed with immortality. She cannot kill herself!"

"Yes, of course," I say. "I'm just dazed."

"It is understandable. You have been through a great deal." He climbs up to my step and pats me on the head.

I respond with a purr. "So why did she plunge a knife into her chest?"

"She wanted you to feel her utter despair."

"How do you know?"

"After you passed out, Nefertiti and I talked through the night.

"What's happened to her?"

"Nothing. She is where you found her."

"And where were you carrying me"

 Silence.

"I'm waiting."

He clears his throat. "I was carrying you to the magic boat. We are going back to ancient Egypt."

"What?! So that's why your head is shaved!"

And it's said cats are devious!

"I would have explained everything once we were on the boat."

"Explain now, or I'm not getting on the boat! Why go back to ancient Egypt?"

"Nefertiti told me that in the thirteenth year of her husband's reign and her first year as co-regent, she had suffered an episode of amnesia. She lost any memory of ten days in the season of Shemu, the night of first to the tenth of the month of Epep. She woke up thinking it was the second of Epep, but she had no recollection of the night before. A few hours later she realized it was in fact the eleventh of Epep."

"Didn't anyone tell her what had happened during those ten days?"

"No, because she never asked. She kept her amnesia a secret. She was afraid her husband might declare her unfit to continue as his co-regent."

"Ah!"

"I am convinced that what erased Nefertiti's memory also made her immortal. If I discover what it was, I might be able to free her from her immortality."

"Have you tried the Entering, as you did to retrieve Elena's lost memory?"

"I did not think it wise. Have you forgotten that I became trapped in her memory and would have stayed there forever had you not managed to pull me out?! The only thing to do now is travel to ancient Egypt in Nefertiti's time and try to discover what happened to her during those ten days."

"You mean, spy on her?"

"Essentially, yes. I have composed a prayer that should steer the boat to the day just prior to the ten days, the last day of the month of Paoni. But it will be extremely difficult to spy on

106

Nefertiti."

"What better spy than a cat? You want my help."

"Yes, Wrappa-Hamen. I need you."

"All right. But why were you carrying me while I was still asleep?"

"I had to act fast. I was afraid Elena might wake up before we left."

"So she doesn't know about your plan."

"I left a letter by her bedside," the High Priest says sheepishly. "It explains everything. We must go to the boat!"

I follow him as he walks up to the attic, goes through the door, and climbs in the boat.

"Let us go inside the cabin," he says.

He opens the basket in which Elena stored his Egyptian garments, and begins to take off his modern clothing, first removing from around his waist a cord with a small bag attached.

"What's in the bag?" I ask.

"I have made sandwiches for us." He takes his skirt and his semitransparent robe out of the basket and quickly puts them on.

"Don't forget the bag!" I say. He puts the cord around his waist, ties it, then leaves the cabin.

I hear him invoke the god Thoth and chant his prayer. The boat begins to move. As always, it first rocks, then spins—

"Don't go!" I hear Elena cry. "Don't go!"

The High Priest hurries back into the cabin. Now the boat is spinning very fast.

"We'll be back!" I yell as loud as I can, hoping Elena can hear me.

But will we? Will I ever see her again, or my beloved little Pharaoh? Oh, High Priest, I hope you know what you're doing.

As always when the magic boat travels through time, I faint.

Chapter 17

"Wrappa-Hamen, Wrappa-Hamen, wake up!"

"What's happened?"

"I think we made it."

What the hell is the High Priest talking about? Then everything comes back to me in a rush.

We're still in the cabin. The boat is rocking gently as if floating on water. We go outside to take a look.

Is this the Nile? It seems so, but where along the river are we?

When my eyes adjust to the bright sunlight, I study the landscape on the near bank. I'm looking east, and I recognize the semicircular cliffs that enclose the valley.

When the Pharaoh and I passed this stretch on our way to Menfi, and he told me about Queen Nefertiti and Pharaoh Akhenaten, there was that nothing left of their city, Akhetaten, but dust and ruins.

What I see now, sandwiched between the river and the cliffs, is the city of Akhetaten at its height. To the left is a monumental white structure with two long jetties extending into the Nile. It must be the Royal Palace.

I take a deep breath. I no longer smell the polluted air of the twenty-first century. I feel reinvigorated. Egypt. My land. How I've missed you! I look at the High Priest. He's wiping a furtive tear from his cheek. I look away to avoid embarrassing him—and to wipe my own tears.

"So, first things first," he says, sighing. "Let me remove the bandage from your head. You look like a study for mummification."

Thanks to you!

He unravels the bandage, none too carefully.

Why is he staring at my head?

"It's not my star?" I ask, panicking. "You didn't ruin my star?"

"No, no, your star is fine. I told you back in New York the wound was just to the side of it. But please do not move. And close your eyes."

The High Priest's fingers are moving around on the top of my head.

What's wrong? My legs begin to shake.

"You can open your eyes now," he says finally, holding a pair of small scissors in his right hand. "I removed the stitches. You did not feel a thing, did you?"

"Am I scarred for life?"

"Of course not," he says in a dismissive tone. "The fur has begun to grow. You head will be fine. And now that you are less likely to attract attention, we can begin our mission."

The Nile is alive with boats, some docking, others leaving. Some of the boats docking carry a cargo of fresh fish, the skins glimmering in the sun. The odor makes me salivate.

"I had better dock the boat there," the High Priest says, pointing at an empty space between two large boats.

"I'll help you."

"No. That will attract even more attention than your bandage. You have to behave like an ordinary cat. Otherwise the authorities might detain us."

"But Nefertiti is here. She'll protect us."

"Wrappa-Hamen, you forget that the Nefertiti we will meet here does not know us."

He's right!

"We have no more time to waste in idle chat. I have to dock the boat. What you can do is practice being an ordinary cat. Stay on all fours and meow instead of talking."

I comply, performing my repertoire of meows while the High Priest docks the boat.

The High Priest in the lead, we walk along the quay.

It's alive with noise and activity. Cargo boat are being loaded or unloaded. Lines of dock workers carry goods to and from the boats like busy ants. Some of the goods deposited on the quay are soon put on backs of donkeys by men working for impatient, loud-mouthed merchants, whose orders mix with loud brays. Other goods the merchants trade between themselves on the spot.

The foreign merchants speak their own language, but laced with Egyptian words. The Egyptian merchants curse them and their cheapness, but with a smile. Egyptians are kind people for the most part, even in business.

Suddenly, a fisherman lays a basket full of fish on top of my right forepaw. I suppress all the colorful human curses I've learned over the years and loudly meow instead.

Unaware of my injury, the High Priest turns to whisper, "Enough practice for now!"

To console myself, I snatch a fish from the basket.

Egyptians revere cats, but, as I've had occasion to note, there are exceptions.

The fisherman kicks me in the rump, and the kick sends me flying past the High Priest.

"What's your hurry?" he asks.

He again takes the lead and walks as if he knows where he's going. He moves so fast I lose sight of him in the crowd. I try picking up his scent, but hundreds of smells fill the air, from pig's manure to sweet incense.

Panic sets in when a child bends down to pet me. "Mother, Mother, look what I've found," he screams with joy to a tall, overweight woman.

"Leave the beast alone. It might belong to someone."

"Please, Mother, let me keep him."

The child pets me so hard I'm pinned down to the ground. I struggle to free myself from his small hands, but they're so strong I can't break his grip. He'd surely let me go if I bite him, but I don't have the heart to do it.

He puts his hands around my stomach and tries to lift me up. Coming to his assistance, his mother takes me out of his hands, holds me tight in hers, and raises me to her chest. "We can't afford keeping a cat as fat as this one," she says laughing. "He'll eat us out of house and home!"

I've never been so offended in my life. Well, I have, but not for a long time. Why doesn't the High Priest come back to look for me? He'd tell this woman I'm a very special cat and she should put me down and apologize to me.

"Oh, Mother, please."

My ears can't believe what they hear next. "All right. We'll take him home."

Just my luck to run into a weak parent!

The only thing to do is to bite hard on one of the woman's

thick biceps. She screams and throws me up into the air.

Aloft, I look for the High Priest. I spot him yards off, elbowing his way through the crowd. But he's headed in the opposite direction. If only it were safe for me to talk, I'd call after him.

What goes up must come down, and I land on a donkey's head. The silly beast takes off like an arrow, braying at the top of his lungs. I dig my claws into his fur and hold on for dear life.

People are moving out of our way, swearing at us both. One voice stands out from the rest. The donkey's owner is hurling curses at me that would make even a veteran soldier blush. I look over my shoulder. He's right behind his donkey.

Just my luck! The man who's threatening to skin me alive is in good physical shape.

Fearing my life is about to be ended, I see what, in the circumstances anyway, is a beautiful sight.

"Wrappa-Hamen," the High Priest says, "I see you have hitched a ride."

I jump off the donkey's head onto his shoulder. "Don't ask questions," I scream. "Run."

Thank the gods, for once he does what he's told. Indeed, he takes off like a professional sprinter. It seems Elena's cooking hasn't completely ruined him.

I no longer hear the donkey's owner cursing me, and when I look over my shoulder, I don't see him chasing us. I guess all he really wanted was his donkey back. It's said of the common folk they readily forgive. But prudence dictates I shouldn't put this to the test by going back to face the man.

The High Priest's running has taken us to a road. On one side are groves of fruit trees and on the other is a barley field.

"You can stop now," I say. "We're out of danger."

He looks around to make sure no one can hear us. He lifts me off his shoulder—a bit too roughly for my taste, but I let it go since he's saved my life—sets me down under a tree, then joins me in the shade.

"How is it that we have not been in ancient Egypt but ten minutes and you are already in trouble?"

"I lost track of you, a child had me pinned down, his mother grabbed me—"

"You are exhibiting symptoms of what in the future will be known as a persecution complex."

"Armchair psychologist!"

"Be silent. Someone is coming."

A group of guards is marching towards us. When they reach our tree, one of them—the leader, I assume—points at me. "Is that your cat?" he asks the High Priest.

"Yes. Why?"

"We're looking for a savage cat that assaulted a woman and then a donkey."

How the facts get twisted!

"My cat has been with me the all time. And look at him. Does he look savage?"

I begin to groom myself, partly to look innocent, but also so I can cover my star with my paw just in case the woman and the donkey's owner have included it in their description.

The guard studies me. I avoid his stare. "You're right. It's just a dumb beast."

"I keep him out of pity."

"Well, if you should see that wild animal, keep away. It's dangerous."

"I will. Thank you for the warning."

When the guards resume marching, the High Priest mumbles, shaking his head, "You are not only paranoid but dangerous."

I'm so relieved the guards are gone I ignore his comment. "Should we move on?" I ask.

"I must rest for a while longer. That run took it out of me."

He closes his eyes. I'm also tired, but too excited to be back in my native land to take a nap. Instead, I study my surroundings.

It's shemu, the harvest season. The High Priest got us here in the right season, but is it the right date? Remembering past mishaps I remain skeptical, but I'll keep it to myself to avoid a lecture on the difficulties of wording prayers precisely.

Laborers are in the field. The reapers are cutting the ripened barley. They hold the heads of grain in one hand and use the other to cut below them with a sickle. "The Aten has been kind," they chant, "the barley has grown, the beer will flow . . ."

112

The reapers are followed by gleaners with baskets. They pick up the heads of grain that have fallen to the ground during the cutting. I remember that the gleaners often squabble. Each gets to keep part of the grain he finds so they compete with one another.

Sure enough, some of the gleaners begin squabbling, and I become reacquainted with some colorful Egyptian curses.

The noise brings the High Priest back to consciousness. "What is that?"

"It's a disagreement over barley. By the way, I'm hungry."

"Shush," he says, looking in the direction of the laborers. "They might hear you."

"Don't worry. They're too busy and too far away."

The High Priest opens the small cloth sack on the cord around his waist and takes out two sandwiches wrapped in foil. He unwraps one of them and places it on the ground in front of me with the foil under it.

I look at him puzzled.

"Sorry, Wrappa-Hamen," he explains. "But you must get used to eating your food on the ground like an ordinary cat."

I wait for him to remove the foil from the other sandwich. When I see it's the same size as mine—being an ordinary cat doesn't shouldn't mean getting smaller portions!—I start eating. Food is food, whether you pick it up with your paws to eat it, or pick it up from the ground with your teeth.

"I've never enjoyed a sandwich so much," I say when I finish.

"It was just ham and cheese," the High Priest. "What made it special was eating it here in our native land."

"I suppose you're right."

He again reaches inside the small sack. I'm hoping to see another sandwich, but it's just a piece of paper. I move closer to him, and he holds the paper under my nose. There's a series of blocks with lettering inside.

"It is an archaeological map of Akhetaten," he explains. "I ripped it out of one of the books in Nefertiti's library. Can you tell from this where we are?"

I study the map for a moment and point at the block labeled the Fields. "We're here."

"Excellent. How did you work it out?"

"Well, I started with the block labeled the Great Palace. It's to our left, which is north. I saw the palace from the boat. When we ran away from the donkey's owner, we headed south of the palace and crossed a stretch of desert between the quay and"—I point to another block on the map—"these Enclosures and Storehouses. Then we turned east onto this road"—I move my claw again —"and ran along the edge of the Fields."

"Well done, Wrappa-Hamen. But you erred by saying 'we ran.' I did the running. You had a ride. Now, commit this map to memory before we eat it."

"Eat it?!"

"I have seen people eat pieces of paper in movies I watch on Elena's television."

Has television turned the High Priest's brain to mush?

"Why do people eat pieces of paper the movies?" I ask, humoring him.

"To destroy the evidence of course."

"What evidence do you wish to destroy?"

"Evidence that we have come from the future. How could we to explain this piece of paper to an ancient Egyptian?"

"Does the word papyrus mean anything to you?!"

"This paper is much finer than papyrus, and on it is a map of the city with words from an unrecognizable language. If we are caught with it, it will raise questions we will not be able to answer."

Makes sense. But it's enough he's shared his concern with me. I don't want him to share the map as well. He can eat it all!

He hasn't mentioned the aluminum foil. "What do people in the movies do when the evidence they want to destroy is used aluminum foil?" I ask him. "Eat it?"

His face turns a hot shade of pink. "Hmm, I did not think of that." He ponders for a few seconds. "We will bury it."

Back in ancient Egypt for less than an hour, and we're polluting the environment already. May the gods forgive us!

"Hey, you," shouts a bare-chested portly man coming towards us. "You're not one of my crew. This is private property. Get going."

Jolted into action, the High Priest crumbles the map and

shoves it in his mouth, then picks the foil up from the ground and crushes it in his fist. By the time the man reaches the tree, we're on our way.

"And don't come back!"

We've gone a hundred paces down the road that skirts the fields when the High Priest starts coughing. He stops walking, doubles over, and spits up bits of paper. Passing by is a caravan of donkeys loaded down with goods. "Some people get drunk while others sweat to make a living," says the man leading the donkeys. "Shame on you. It serves you right to be sick." As if agreeing, one of the donkeys lets out a long bray.

"Wrappa-Hamen," the High Priest begins, pausing to spit out another bit of paper, "if we ever get back to the future and you see me turn on the television, please hit me on the head."

"Gladly," I say under my breath.

Chapter 18

When the High Priest recovers enough to walk, we continue along the road. We pass one field after another. Some are filled with laborers harvesting the crop, just like the barley field behind the tree where we rested. Others are swollen with crops yet to be harvested. Several are covered with grazing animals.

If we keep going, we'll come upon the market. According to the map I've memorized, it comes after the fields and spreads southwards . . .

Hundreds of voices and almost as many smells herald the market well before we see it. Still feeling ill from swallowing the map, the High Priest has kept silent. The prospect of a market revives him. "We might not get another opportunity. Do you want to go?"

I've been hoping he'd ask. I love markets, and—who knows? —I might be lucky enough to find food.

"Yes," I reply enthusiastically.

The High Priest picks me up and sets me on his shoulder. "I do not want to lose you in the crowd again," he whispers in my ear.

From my vantage point, I see that the market is spread over a large area. We join the throng seeking bargains—women with children, women alone, women with servants, men with children, men alone, men with servants. All except the very young carry sacks or baskets filled with goods to trade or goods received in trade.

There are animal pens, reed stalls worked by merchants of both sexes, and reed mats on which the poorer merchants display their goods. In the stalls, the goods are spread over low wooden stands or hung from hooks placed on the cross bar.

We pass a stall with rolls of linen on the stands and shawls hanging from the hooks. The next stall belongs to a sandal maker. He's putting the finishing touches to a pair of sandals while a boy, his son most probably, is keeping a watchful eye on a potential buyer, or perhaps potential thief, who, to get a better look, is twisting and turning one of many pairs of sandals hanging from a hook.

"Go to your left," I whisper to the High Priest. "That stall has

116

toys."

Of the many toys on display, most are dolls. They range from finely carved, lifelike wooden dolls to simple ones—just wooden paddles with heads, or simpler yet, dolls made of reed and dressed in coarse cloth. Some are painted, others barely touched by color. Some have beads in their hair or are decked with jewelry, fake of course.

A young mother whose little girl has chosen a painted paddle doll hands three eggs and a loaf of bread to the merchant. He gives the doll directly to the child, then turns his attention to us. "Oh, what a beautiful cat you have there. I have a toy cat that's quite special."

The man points. The toy cat is sitting among balls of painted leather used for jostling, linen rolls, and other items received in trade, including the eggs and the loaf of bread left by the young mother.

When the High Priest shows no interest, the merchant picks up the toy and shoves it under his nose. The cat is carved out of wood, covered with a reddish patina, and has a string that goes through the head and mouth. The High Priest takes the toy from the merchant and studies it, turning it in his hands. He pulls on the string and the cat's mouth opens.

Is he merely being polite, or is he actually interested?

"A nice little toy," the merchant says. "It'd make a child very happy."

"I will take it."

I can't believe my ears. The High Priest has nothing to offer in exchange. But it's nice of him to have thought of getting me a gift.

"It will take it back home as a gift for my son."

Of course, it's for the little Pharaoh. But how can the High Priest bargain for it?

"What do you have to trade?" the merchant asks. "The toy is worth—"

"My cat. He is very special. He performs tricks."

The High Priest wants to trade me for the toy! He's gone crazy! I dig my claws into my demented friend's shoulder.

"Of course, I do not mean to give him to you, only his tricks," he explains. "They will draw people to your stall. That should

117

increase your trade."

Better. But what does he mean by tricks?

The merchant seems to be reading my mind. "What kind of tricks does he do?"

"Clear the table, and I, that is, he, will demonstrate." With the table cleared, the High Priest takes me off his shoulder and places me on it. "If I pull his tail, he opens his mouth and sticks his tongue out."

How humiliating!

The High Priest grabs my tail and gives it a tug. I think of the little Pharaoh, of how happy the toy will make him. I open my mouth and stick my tongue out.

The merchant claps. "Come, everyone, come," he shouts. "You have a treat in store for you. Come and see a cat perform tricks." Some people move over to the stall, and the merchant says, "Do it again."

The High Priest again yanks on my tail. I again think of the little the Pharaoh's happiness and stick my tongue out.

"Ohh, Uhhh, Ahhh," cry parents and children alike.

"What else can he do?" asks the merchant, excited.

He's rubbing his hands together in anticipation. The more tricks I can do, the more trade he can do. But I think that was enough, and I'm sure the High Priest will tell him so—

"He can count with his tail."

He'll pay for this if it's the last thing I do!

"Three," he says to me.

What does he mean by counting with my tail?

The only thing to do is swish my tail from side to side three times. There are more exclamations of wonder from the onlookers, and some of the children begin to pester their parents to buy me.

"Can he do anything else?" the greedy merchant asks.

Surely, I've done enough to earn the toy cat. Surely, the High Priest will tell him so—

"He can jump through a circle."

The High Priest puts his arms forward, clasps his hands together to make a circle, then tilts it so I can jump through.

"Jump," he commands.

I clench my teeth to stop myself from cursing out loud. All

thought of the little Pharaoh's happiness has been replaced by humiliation over the loss of my dignity. I jump—not through the circle, but down from the table.

Little hands try to grab me, but I'm too fast. I scurry through the legs of both adults and children, tripping someone in the process. I hear a crash, then screams and curses. I know what fell —the stall and its toys—and on whom—the merchant and his customers.

I keep going. The High Priest is by my side, one hand holding the toy cat. "We had better split up," he cries.

I'm quick to follow his advice. While he keeps running in a straight line, I veer to the left. When I look back over my shoulder, he's already lost himself in the crowd. I try to do likewise.

The gods only know whether the merchant and his customers have alerted the guards. Maybe we're already being pursued, and maybe by the same guards that approached us at the tree.

So much for the High Priest's instruction not to call attention to ourselves!

Minutes later, my lungs ready to burst, I slow to a walk and find myself behind two merchants, one thin and young, the other plump and middle aged. They're talking about shipments.

"I'm ruined," the thin young merchant says, breathing heavily. "I invested all I had in the shipment from Nubia. Now I've been told the ship caught fire. I'm ruined."

"You got too greedy," the other one says.

"But, Seti, what I did was follow your advice."

"I didn't force you, did I?"

"No, no." The thin young merchant wipes the sweat from behind his neck. "But you were so positive I should take a chance. You said it would be the chance of my life."

"It's not my fault it turned out to be a bad investment."

"I was wondering . . . Could you bail me out?"

"Bail you out?" Seti says with disdain. "I can't afford to help fools."

The thin young merchant stops, shaking. I stop too.

"I'm ruined, ruined," he cries. "My children will suffer. Won't you help me for their sake?"

Seti continues walking and soon disappears from view. I feel sorry for the thin young merchant. His eyes are closed, but I see tears streaking down his face. He starts hitting his head with his fists, and I bump into his legs to startle him.

"Are you homeless?" he asks, massaging his head. "That's what I'm going to be after I finish with my creditors. Or, I should say, when they finish with me."

He bends forward and tickles me under my chin. I purr to let him know I like it, but he stops abruptly. "I can't go home to face my wife and child . . . There's only one thing for me to do."

He looks about nervously, wringing his hands. What does he plan to do?

"I'll do away with myself," he says with determination and runs away from me.

I should look for the High Priest, or at least not make it any harder for him to find me, but how can I not try to save the poor merchant?

Without further ado, I give chase. And what a chase! The merchant, believe it or not, is faster than I am. Nothing gives a man more strength than a firm resolution, even if that resolution is wrong.

I meow loudly, and he turns. "Go away, cat, go away," he yells.

The streets are crowded. I keep losing track of him only to have him reappear. Where the street is level, I see only his running feet. Where it's uphill, I see all of him. He gains too much ground, and I lose him for good. Desperate, I try to pick up his scent. But there are too many smells.

The chase has brought me back to the quay. In the distance, I see the donkey whose head I jumped on and his owner. Just my luck. They must be on the quay all day long.

Making an about-face, I suddenly realize where my suicidal merchant has gone. He's thrown himself in the Nile!

I get closer to the edge of the quay and look out on the river for signs of a drowning man. There he is, being swept away by the current. I meow as loud as I can.

Has he heard me? He seems to look back, but I'm not sure.

I jump in and swim towards him. He's very far away. I can't

keep swimming at this pace. I won't have enough strength left to drag him back. In fact, between the running and the swimming, I don't have very much strength left now.

I force myself to go a little further only to realize I'm too weak to swim back to the quay. I take a few desperate strokes, then shut my eyes.

Once long ago when I was drowning the Pharaoh saved me, but now . . . My life is about to end. It's been a strange and wonderful life. Thank you, Bastet, for giving me human powers! You also said I was going to live a long time. It's been only . . . but I'm not complaining. And dying alone in the middle of the Nile is still better than being killed by a bus in New York City.

Egypt has seen my birth. Now she will see my death.

Nefertiti, forgive me for failing you. And Elena, Alexander, Gato-Hamen, remember me . . .

Chapter 19

"Do you think he'll live?" a woman's voice asks.

I'm too weak to open my eyes

"If he dies," says a voice I recognize as the young merchant's, "I have but myself to blame."

"My dear husband, don't be ridiculous. You did your best to save him."

I feel someone's breath on my right ear. "Please live," he whispers. I stir.

"Oh, look he's moved," his wife cries with joy.

"We've both been saved!"

I cough up a little water and, feeling better, open my eyes. How long have I been unconscious?

The oil lamps are lit, and when I look up at the windows set high in the walls, I see that the sky is filled with stars. I've been unconscious all day!

I'm in a large square room with a high ceiling held up by four painted wooden pillars in the form of palm trees. The lofty ceiling and the clerestory windows tell me I'm in the main room at the center of the house. The room is quite airy, having at least two doorways in each wall.

I'm lying on a settee placed against one of the walls and covered with pillows. Husband and wife are sitting on either side of me, bent over me. I wish I could thank the husband for saving my life. Instead, I lick the hand he's rested under my chin.

"Praise the Goddess Bastet, protector of cats," the wife says.

Yes!

"I'll have Kaya fetch some fresh bread and milk from the kitchen. I'll be right back."

"My wife doesn't know I'm ruined and tried to kill myself," the young merchant whispers to me when she's gone. "She thinks I'm a hero who risked his life to save a drowning cat. If you hadn't followed me and almost drowned in the process, I'd be dead now. And my family would be left with no one to protect them. By saving you, I've saved myself and them."

He shakes his head at the irony, then looks into my eyes and continues whispering. "I don't know why I'm telling you these things. But I like to think you understand what I'm saying to you."

If he only knew!

I look around. Elena would like this room. She always complains about the clutter in our home in New York, and like any ancient Egyptian room, this one's sparsely furnished——rugs here and there, small tables for the oil lamps, painted chests against three of the walls, and, against the fourth wall, the white-washed brick settee I'm lying on.

And given her artistic nature, Elena would also appreciate how the room is alive with color—the pure white walls, the red pillars with the bright green palm leaves touching the blue ceiling, the vivid colors in the pillows on the settee and in the rugs on the red tiled floor, and the medley of the fresh-cut flowers in the faience vase in the center of the room between the four pillars, in the small sunken space where a brazier might sit during the winter.

The young merchant's wife comes back into the room carrying a tray. "Here we are. I brought a little honey as well."

She sits down, setting the tray on her lap. There's a loaf of bread, a jar of milk, and a pot of honey. She dips her index finger in the pot, then brings it to my mouth. I raise my head a little and lick all the honey off.

She smiles. A beautiful smile on a beautiful face moisturized with precious oils, aglow even in the near darkness of the room.

"Look how he stares at me," she says. "It's the same stare I get from men in the street when I pass by."

"He's a cat with good taste," her husband says, laughing.

"A regular ladies' cat, you are," she says, kissing me on my head.

I feel myself getting red under my fur and purr madly.

"The children," he says, "will be happy to have a cat."

That's twice today someone has tried to adopt me!

I get up on my fours and jump off the stool. The effort makes me cough, but instead of water a fur ball comes out. Husband and wife both laugh.

"I guess that means he's completely recovered," he says.

She picks up the saucer of milk and sets it on the floor in front of me, then breaks off a piece of the bread and crumbles it with both hands, letting the crumbs splash into the milk. Some droplets of milk land on my nose, but I don't mind.

"Go on, eat," she says.

She doesn't have to say it twice. I consume the milk-soaked bread with gusto.

"The poor beast," he says. "The Aten only knows when he ate last."

As I lick my whiskers, I feel a pang of guilt. The last time I ate was with the High Priest, and he probably hasn't had anything to eat since.

The High Priest! He must be desperate by now. He's probably thinking he's never going to see me again . . .

"We'd better retire," the wife says. "It's been a strenuous day for you, and I have a lot to do tomorrow before I take the children to see grandma."

"I'll come with you. I'll visit a while, then go to work."

"You heard what the doctor said! After the ordeal you've had, you need to rest. He's given me a sleeping potion for you. Tomorrow you'll sleep late, and spend the rest of the day relaxing!"

"You're right of course. I'm exhausted."

"I wish I could stay home with you, but it'll break my mother's heart if I don't go. She's been very sad since my father's passing. The children will cheer her up . . . I'll be back by sunset."

I won't leave till she returns!

A large woman enters the room. She's wearing a plain white tunic. Semitransparent, it makes her large breasts almost visible. Her makeup is exaggerated, but it suits her.

I like the woman. I like humans who enjoy their food, and, judging by her size, she certainly enjoys hers.

"So the pussum survived," she says, looking me over.

"Indeed he has, Kaya," the wife says. "Praise the Aten!"

"Praise the Aten!"

"We're retiring now, Kaya . . . You go ahead," she says to her husband. "I'll bar the doors tonight."

"Thank you, dear."

His wife gets up, then helps him up. He leaves by one of the doorways on either side of the settee.

"May the Aten protect you during sleep, Kaya," he calls back.

124

"May the Aten protect you, your wife, and your children during sleep."

"I'll bar the front door first," the wife says. "Kaya, leave by the side door. I'll bar it once you've gone. The cat can sleep where he is."

All of a sudden there's a loud thud followed by a muffled curse from the young merchant.

"He didn't take a lamp, did he?" his wife says, shaking her head. "Typical man!" she adds, quickly taking one and hurrying after him.

Kaya stares down at me, and I give her a pathetic look, hoping she'll take me with her.

"You're sleeping with me in the servants' quarters," she says.

Thank you, Bastet! In the the servants' quarters I'll be near the kitchen!

Kaya leans forward and picks me up as if I were a feather, not the big cat I am.

We leave the main room through a doorway in the wall opposite the settee, and enter a rectangular hall, also pillared and sparsely furnished. Kaya takes a lit oil lamp from a recess in the wall. With one hand holding me and the other the lamp, she kicks open one of the double doors, and we enter the courtyard surrounding the house.

I recognize the dome-shaped structures as granaries. Kaya walks alongside them to the back of the house, turns the corner, walks toward a long outbuilding. My nose tells me the kitchen is at the far end!

Kaya enters the servants' quarters at the middle. Her room is small with just a bed and a woven basket to store her clothing. On top of the basket is a small open box filled with simple faience jewelry, little jars, and a palette on which to grind minerals and mix the powder to be used as eye makeup.

Kaya sets me down on her bed and puts the oil lamp she's been carrying in a recess in the wall behind the head of the bed. On the wall facing the bed is a mural of a large cat with a silvery coat and blue eyes perched on a tree limb. He looks very much like yours truly!

"Do you like it? I painted it. It's my imaginary cat."

What does she mean?

"When I was a little girl," she explains as she begins to undress, "I wanted so much to own a cat. But my parents were poor. Another mouth to feed would've been too much of a burden for them. So I decided to invent a cat. And at night when everyone was asleep I'd tell him all my problems and dreams."

Naked, she slips under the cover, grabs me, and pulls me under as well. "And now you have come alive!"

Yes. One could say I'm her dream come true!

"When I was growing up I wanted to become an artist, but art workshops are open only to boys, boys whose families could afford it."

Considering the skill with which the cat was painted, she would have made a very good artist.

"But I've been fortunate," she says just as I'm beginning to feel sorry for her. "I'm happy here. The work isn't too hard and I'm well-treated."

"Will you shut up in there?" someone nearby says. "I'm trying to get some sleep."

Kaya lowers her voice. "That'll be Maya. She's the youngest servant here. She has no manners. But it is getting late. Let's sleep."

I respond with a yawn.

Kaya reaches for the oil lamp. Suddenly it's dark. When my vision adjusts, I see her rub her eyes with the back of her hands.

Tears?

She falls asleep. But I can't stop thinking about the strange day I've had.

Kaya rolls over to my side, puts an arm around me, and pulls me against her breasts. They're as soft as butter and smell like freshly baked honey cakes dipped in milk. I sink my head in them. Kaya begins to snore, but I don't mind.

I sleep like a kitten.

Chapter 20

My head searches for Kaya's "pillows," but they're gone. I open my eyes. Sunlight seeps through the window. Kaya is nowhere to be seen. The young merchant's wife is talking in the courtyard, sounding very animated.

I stretch, give my face and body a perfunctory lick, then jump out of bed. I go over to the basket under the window, jump on it and up onto the windowsill to see what's going on.

The wife is talking to two young servant girls. ". . . and make sure you do the rugs today. And don't do what you did last time and take all the rugs out at once. When you beat the dust out of one it goes into another. Take one rug out at a time, hang it in the yard, beat the dust out, then take it down and put it back inside. Understood?!"

She gives the girls a benign smile and they nod.

"Go then," she says, "and, one of you, tell the stable man to keep an eye on the pregnant donkey. She's do any day now."

As the girls leave, the wife notices me.

"Kaya told me you slept all night," she says, giving me the same benign smile she gave the girls. "I'm not surprised. You almost died yesterday . . . Well, now you can make up for the nocturnal prowling you didn't do."

She raises herself on the tips of her toes, stretches a hand, and tickles me under the chin. "Enjoy yourself. I'm off."

Enjoy myself I will!

I jump down into the courtyard and, walking past the servants' quarters, follow the smell of baked bread and mutton stew to the kitchen. I'm salivating at the thought of what awaits me inside when I have a sudden need to relieve myself. By now, I've reached the other side of the house. I turn the corner and continue till I find the perfect spot by the geese and ducks pen.

The aroma from the kitchen enhances the smell of their droppings, while the latter diminishes the smell of the food . . .

I've just peed and I'm about to poop when fierce barking behind me shrinks my anal sphincter. I turn to face a huge spotted hound!

I take off, running like the wind with him barking and chasing after me. The walls that surround the estate are too high for me to jump over. I ignore the trees, not wanting to get stuck up in one.

Within moments, I make up for the nocturnal prowling I missed. I pass a garden, a pool, a chapel, the gate to the estate—which, as luck would have it, is closed—the granaries, a stable, the servants' quarters, and end up back at the geese and ducks pen with the hound right behind me.

I can't outrun the hound, and he won't give up. The only thing to do is turn and fight—

"Tiny, come here!" an old man yells, stepping out of the kitchen. He tears a piece off the loaf of bread he's holding. The hound goes to his side, and the man gives him the piece of bread.

Then he tears off another piece and holds it out to me. "Come. Don't be afraid. Tiny loves cats. He's just a puppy. He wants to play with you."

Tiny? Never was a dog so misnamed! He's the size of a young bull and has the testicles of one. And he's just a puppy? What will he be like grown up?

The offer of the piece of bread is too alluring to refuse. I approach the man with trepidation. Tiny stays put, panting and salivating, and I take the bread in my mouth . . .

Then it happens! Tiny is all over me. He pins me to the ground, and I'm being licked and slobbered over. Biting and scratching a puppy, even an over-sized one, is beneath me, but a well-placed jab isn't. I give him one on the nose, and he gets off me.

Only now do I remember that dogs are not allowed in kitchens since food is prepared on the floor, the cooks squatting or kneeling.

I run into the kitchen. Tiny barks in complaint, but dares not follow me with his master watching.

I find myself in the area of the kitchen, shaded by a palm leaf roof, where jars, bowls, and provisions are kept. In the part of the kitchen reserved for cooking—roofless as in all the many Egyptian kitchens I've had the pleasure to visit—I see Kaya using a long wooden spoon to stir the mutton stew simmering in a clay pot on a cylindrical clay stove.

The smell of mutton cooked with garlic, cumin, and onions is overwhelming!

"Meow."

"Oh, you startled me," Kaya says turning. "Well, it's about time you got up. It's past midday."

"Meow."

"I know what you want," she says, moving into the roofed area of the kitchen.

From a recess in the wall she takes a pitcher and bowl, comes back to me, sets a saucer on the floor, and pours milk from the pitcher. I begin to lap it up. It's still warm from the cow's udders.

A cow moos in the stable. Is she the one whose milk I'm enjoying?

The second bowl of milk Kaya gives me is even better because she's added pieces of bread.

Full and satisfied, I groom myself, licking off Tiny's sticky drool, while Kaya squats by my side, mashing boiled chick peas in a large bowl, to which, at intervals, she adds drops of sesame oil.

Half an hour later, I have just the tip of my tail left to groom, and Kaya is now sweeping the floor, when my host, the thin young merchant, appears at the door. "Kaya, what's that wonderful smell?"

"I'm making mutton stew for supper. Your wife thought it'd help you regain your strength."

"Actually, I'm feeling quite well. I've never slept so soundly for so long in my life."

"You slept longer than the cat!"

"I'm going to work after all," he says. "I should be back before my wife returns." Bending down to pat me on the head, he adds, "Make sure he's is well taken care of."

"Don't worry about him. He's being treated like royalty."

Indeed I am!

"Have a good afternoon, Kaya," he says as he leaves.

As much as I'd like to stay here with Kaya, I have to look after my host. He said he'd learned his lesson, but what if despair overwhelms him again?

I follow him. When we get to the gate, the gatekeeper turns out to be the old man who gave me the bread. Tiny is sleeping, curled up like a cat, inside the gatekeeper's lodge.

"Good afternoon, Sabef," says the thin young merchant.

Sabef bows slightly and opens the gate. As he's about to close it, I sneak through, and he tries to shoo me back in. My host turns, sees me, and gives me a thoughtful stare. "Let him be, Sabef. I can use the company."

Side by side we walk, passing rows and rows of merchant villas hidden from view by mud-brick walls the height of two men. I know there are villas behind the walls because I can read the names and titles carved on the lintel of each gate.

We make our way out of the residential area into the market where I was yesterday. It seems even busier today. I look for the High Priest. But after a while I give up. It's like trying to find a particular ant in an ants' nest.

My host walks further into the market than the High Priest and I did. We pass animal pens. The oinking, braying, mooing, clucking, and bellowing are deafening. The smell of manure is sickening. Mercifully, my host walks fast, and we're soon in a calmer, less smelly part of the market.

He stops at a stand selling rugs. Two boys inside are piling another rolled-up carpet on top of a stack.

"Good afternoon, Tij," they say in unison.

I finally know my host's name!

"Good afternoon, boys."

"We've heard the good news," one of them says. "We're glad for you."

"What are you talking about? What good news?"

"You mean you haven't heard? It's all over the quay. Your boat arrived this morning. It was Seti's boat that went up in smoke. Aren't you happy?"

What I hear next surprises me. "How can I rejoice at another man's bad luck?"

Tij is, indeed, a man of honor. The young men look down in embarrassment.

"We just thought it was good news," says the one who told him.

"I'm sorry. I know you meant well . . . Have you made today's deliveries?" Tij asks, changing the subject.

"We did. First thing this morning!"

"You did well."

130

The boys haven't seen me yet, so when I jump on the stack of rugs I startle them. I didn't intend to. I only wanted my presence acknowledged.

"Where's he come from?" asks the boy who hasn't spoken yet.

"From heaven," Tij says.

The boys look at each other, then laugh. They probably think he's teasing them.

Tij comes over to me. The stack of rugs I'm sitting on has raised me high enough to look him directly in the eyes. "Meow."

He understands what I mean. "I'll miss you too."

I'll miss you, Tij, your kind wife, and most of all Kaya. But you no longer need me to look after you, and I must find the High Priest.

I jump down from the stack of rugs and walk away, telling myself not to look back. But when I reach a corner, that's exactly what I do.

Tij is watching me.

"Thank you," he yells.

Don't mention it.

I turn the corner.

Alone on the road outside the market I begin to worry. What if I can't find the High Priest?

As I'm pondering, a scrawny cat comes up to me. "You look well fed. Where do you get your food?"

I tell him I've left an opening for a cat at the home of a rug merchant and his family. It's not too far from here, and he'll be welcomed. I add that the bull, I mean dog, looks frightening, but is a pussycat, so to speak.

He seems skeptical, but I reassure him and give him directions.

"I know where that is. I can take a short cut." He eyes me suspiciously. "How come you don't want the job any more? Is there something wrong with the place?"

I consider telling him the truth about myself, but think better of it. It'd sound so fantastic he'd consider me a lunatic and run off. I don't want him to lose the chance of a lifetime—a good home, a nice family, and best of all Kaya.

"I found something better."

"I see. Well, thanks for the tip, brother."

He disappears before I can reply, "You're welcome."

Once my brother has had a taste of his new life, he's bound to ask himself if it's possible to have something better? But unless he's a fool, and he didn't strike me as one, he'll stop wondering about my good fortune and enjoy his.

Alone again, I decide to return to the quay. The High Priest might be waiting for me on the magic boat.

Just then, who should be walking up the road but the woman whose arm I bit when she was trying to cat-nap me! Unluckily, she sees me too. "It's the cat that assaulted me!" she yells at the top of her lungs.

I turn around to flee in the other direction only to see two guards marching down the street toward me.

"Help!" she yells repeatedly.

The guards break into a run. I race back into the market and almost collide with a caravan of donkeys leaving the market with big baskets on their backs. I jump on the donkey last in line, lift the cover off a basket, get in on top of a malodorous mess, and put the cover back on behind me.

Through the weave of the basket I see the two guards approach the head of the caravan.

"Hey, you," one of them shouts to the man leading the donkeys. "Have you seen a large silvery gray cat running by?"

"I've seen lots of gray donkeys," he replies. "But no, I haven't seen a gray cat . . . You can ask my donkeys if they have," he adds, laughing.

"Watch your smart mouth, donkey man. It might just land you in jail."

The guards walk the length of the caravan, one on either side. They pass my donkey and, finding nothing, extend their search to the market, which by now the caravan has left behind.

I intended to go to the quay to look for the High Priest, but the caravan is moving east towards the populated area. I recognize buildings I passed this morning with the young merchant as we made our way to the market. I play with the idea of leaving my hiding place, but prudence counsels otherwise.

Besides, the malodorous mess I'm sitting on is dried fish, and I'm very hungry. There's no sense in passing up an opportunity for a snack, malodorous as it might be. I grab a fish and give it a bite.

Phew! Salted fish. Still, better than no fish at all.

I chew and swallow, and within minutes my throat is parched. I curse my gluttony till I'm interrupted by men shouting. It's the police. Carrying batons and short forked sticks, they're trying to clear the wide road we've been crossing.

Some are polite. "Please make way for your king and his queen."

Others are very rude. "Move out of the way, you miserable creatures!"

People are scurrying to the sides of the road. The old ones are helped by the younger, and the very young are scooped up by their parents. Everyone is moving except the donkeys in the caravan. They're not budging from the middle of the road.

The poor donkey man pulls on the rope attached to the lead donkey's neck, but the beast stubbornly refuses to move. When he gets whacked on the ass by a police baton, he lets out a loud bray and takes off. The rest of the donkeys follow.

The donkey man won't let go of the rope and is dragged along. Cursing donkeys as much as he is, I'm bounced left and right, back and forth.

As all of this is unfolding, the royal chariot approaches preceded by more police carrying batons and short forked-sticks. Pharaoh Akhenaten and Queen Nefertiti stand side by side, erect and still like statues, their gaze fixed in front of them.

Nefertiti wears the same tall blue flat-topped headdress she does in her famous bust. Given life by the wind, the colorful streamers fastened to the back of it flutter behind her like long wings. In the bright daylight, the gold flaring cobra above her brow shines like a small sun.

Both she and her husband wear a wide collar necklace made of gold. Nefertiti has on a long white sleeveless dress, Akhenaten a white knee-length skirt. His chest is unclad, and he's holding the reins.

Their gold jewelry and their chariot, made of electrum, are ablaze in the sun. The royal figures are illuminated as if they themselves were made of such precious metals.

When the royal chariot has passed and the donkey man has regained control of his beasts, I hear a variety of comments.

"Dirty police!"

"Those crazy donkeys almost trampled me!"

"Our queen is so beautiful!"

Yes, Nefertiti is beautiful! She was beautiful even when she was trying to persuade me to kill her thousands of years ago, or I should say—from now?

"I hope you've learned your lesson," says the donkey man to the lead donkey. "Next time you don't obey, you're going to get a whack from me."

But then he slides his hand affectionately down one of the donkey's long ears all the way to his snoot. The donkey bobs his head up and down and gives his master a nudge.

There's love there!

Chapter 21

Leaving the populated area behind us, we enter the desert and go toward the cliffs. The heat makes me drowsy, but the thirst brought on by the salted fish is so strong it's keeping me awake.

We've been in the desert about half an hour when we approach a brick-walled village. On the lintel over the gate it says Workmen's Village. I've been to such a place before. Masons and artisans live here with their families. They work for the Royal House on the royal tombs and the tombs of high-ranking officials.

As we go through the gate, a group of men cheer the donkey man, and he in turn waves to them. A short stocky man leaves the group and walks towards us. "Good afternoon, Tashi," he says, giving the donkey man a slap on the shoulder. "What do you have for us this week?"

"Good afternoon to you, Kush. I've brought dry fish, lentils, beans, and beer."

"Beer! Bless you! Last week you didn't bring any. The workers were upset, and the guards at the royal tomb were furious. When I bring them their food and there's no beer, they threaten me with their staves."

"I'm sorry," Tashi says, "but it wasn't my fault."

"I know," Kush says, giving him another slap on the shoulder. "It's the Royal House that's to blame. But let's be grateful that this week we'll all have our beer!"

"Tutu, my son," he calls out to a younger man, "go and get your brother and unload the donkeys."

Tutu is short and stocky like his father. He disappears inside a house only to reappear within a few seconds with his brother at his side.

Tashi leads his caravan closer to the house, and the brothers begin to unload the donkeys, singing happily, probably anticipating a bowl of beer when they finish the job. They get to my donkey and pick up the basket I'm hiding in.

"Tashi," says Tutu or his brother, I'm not sure which, "what do you have in here? Stones?"

"Just dried fish. Here, I'll show you." The cover of the basket is lifted, and I'm looking up at Tashi. "You must be the gray cat the guards were after."

I've seen how kindly he treats his donkeys. I know he won't hurt me, but recoil instinctively.

"Don't be afraid," he reassures me.

In the meantime, Kush and the two brothers have joined him. Now I have four pairs of eyes staring at me. I'm preparing to leap out of the basket and run off, but Kush, anticipating my move, reaches in, grabs me by the scruff of the neck, and pulls me out.

"A nice roasted cat will complement the beer," he says. He caresses his belly and laughs.

I know he's only joking, but it's a while before my heartbeat returns to normal.

Kush hoists me onto his free arm and lets go of my neck, holding me like a baby, then looks into the basket and rummages inside with his free hand. He seems to be searching for something in particular.

"Aha! I knew he'd have tried to eat one." He pulls out the fish I've bitten into and dangles it in front of me. "You must be dying of thirst, you silly beast."

I try to meow, but my throat is so dry I can manage only a pathetic bleat. Everyone laughs.

"Let's go inside and have a bowl of beer," Kush says.

"Good idea," the others say in unison.

We enter the house, which is really a large storeroom.

Ah, I see. Kush oversees the food supply for the village.

"Sit," he says to Tashi, pointing to the benches made of mud bricks. "Give your tired bones a rest."

Tashi sits. So do the brothers.

"What do you think you're doing?" Kush says to them. "Don't you have work to do? You'll get your beer later like everybody else."

"But, but . . ." complain his sons.

"No buts."

They get up and, looking downcast, go back outside. Kush hands me to Tashi, who sets me on his lap.

"They're good sons," Kush says. "But they like their beer too much!"

From one of the jars Tashi's donkeys carried, he pours beer

136

into two large bowls.

Like father, like sons?

He hands Tashi a bowl, but doesn't join him on the bench. "I'll be back," he says, putting his bowl down.

He walks around the storeroom, searching. He comes back holding a smaller bowl, sits beside Tashi, and puts it on the bench. He takes me by the scruff of the neck and sets me down on the bench, then picks up his bowl and pours beer in the smaller one.

"Well, aren't you thirsty?" he asks when I hesitate.

I start to lap up the beer. I'd forgotten the peculiar taste of Egyptian beer! Slightly sour and bitter.

I finish and look at the two men. They're wiping their mouths with the backs of their hands.

"That was very refreshing, Kush," says Tashi.

"How about some more?"

"Don't mind if I do."

Tashi tries to hand Kush his bowl.

"No need," Kush says, getting up. "I'll bring the jar over."

When he finishes pouring more beer in their two bowls, I meow and he pours more in mine.

As I'm lapping it up, I feel a pang of guilt. Is the High Priest thirsty? I try to make myself believe he isn't and resume lapping till my bowl is empty.

Three more times, Kush refills his bowl, Tashi's, and mine. At least, I think it's three times. After my third bowl of beer, I'm convinced the High Priest isn't thirsty. After the fourth, I'll bet my life on it . . .

Kush has moved closer to Tashi, as if to tell him a secret. My ears prick up. About the only part of me that can move.

"I have something . . . hic . . . strange to tell you," Kush says quietly.

"I'm . . . hic . . . listening," Tashi says.

"The men working on the . . . hic . . . Royal Tomb tell me that just before they quit for the day a woman arrives. She's dressed like a peasant, but the guards let her enter. When the workers return to the tomb at . . . hic . . . dawn, they see her leave."

"Do they know who the woman is or why . . . hic . . . she goes into the tomb?"

"No."

"Could they ask the . . . hic . . . guards?"

"They're afraid they'd . . . hic . . . be accused of spying."

"I see," Tashi, says nodding. "It's strange about . . . hic . . . the woman."

"Very."

"Yes," Tashi says, nodding some more.

His nodding is making me dizzy. I look away, afraid I might spill my guts all over the place. What would my drinking buddies think of me then?

The men fall silent, pondering the mystery . . .

"I should . . . hic . . . go home," Tashi says, getting up. Kush also gets up, but is too wobbly to stand and sits back down.

"Steady, steady," says Tashi, putting his hand on his friend's shoulder. "No need to get up for me. Goodbye. May the Aten look after you and may your . . . hic . . . beer jars never be empty." He looks down at me. "And you. Stay out of harm's way."

Tashi pulls the door closed behind him.

"Goodbye . . . hic," Kush manages to say, just before closing his eyes and slumping forward.

Here I am, alone with—"hic . . . hic"—a drunk.

And my curiosity! Who is the peasant woman Kush mentioned to Tashi, and what does she do in the Royal Tomb? The only way to find out is to be there myself when she is. But how do I get there?

I hatch what's surely a drunken plan. Were I sober, I'd never jump off the bench, get up on my hinds legs, somewhat unsteadily, and shout in Kush's ear, "Are you asleep?"

"No," he says, stirring. "Tashi, . . . hic . . . you're back?"

"It's not Tashi. It's Wrappa-Hamen."

Kush opens his eyes and, seeing me standing in front of him, sits bolt upright, before sliding off the bench unto the floor. His back against the bench, he shakes his head again and again in disbelief.

"Haven't you . . . hic . . . heard a cat talk before?" I ask.

"You can't fool me," Kush replies. "Whenever I'm very drunk, a donkey . . . hic . . . talks to me. He's an hallucination. So are you."

"I wasn't an hallucination . . . hic . . . when you poured beer for me."

"No, but you weren't . . . hic . . . talking then."

I walk around on my hind legs. "Can the donkey do that?"

"No, he just talks."

"I bet I know . . . hic . . . what he tells you. You cheat the workers out of their beer."

"How do you know?"

When I do something wrong I hear Elena's voice inside my head. In fact I hear it now. "Wrappa-Hamen, you should be ashamed! In ancient Egypt on a vital mission and you get drunk!" Amazing how a cat might time travel through millennia, but not escape his conscience!

Kush's talking donkey appears to him whenever he gets drunk on beer that should have gone to his workers. But if I told him he wouldn't understand. "I know many things," I say instead.

"That's what the donkey says."

"What will convince you I'm not . . . hic . . . an hallucination?"

"Do something real."

"All right, then. Get up and stand . . . hic . . . with your back to the bench."

It takes him a while, but he obeys.

"What are you going to do?"

"You'll see."

Standing on the bench on my hind legs, I swing one leg back as far as it'll go—I'm at just the right height—and, with all my strength, bring it forward to connect with his fat ass.

For a drunken man, Kush yells loudly. "You're not an hallucination!" He turns to me and gets down on his knees. "But you're not a real cat either. A cat can't walk and talk like a human, or kick so hard . . . hic . . . Oh, you're a god . . ."

How I wish Elena and the High Priest could hear him!

"Yes . . . . hic . . . And you'll get another kick if you don't obey me."

"I'll do anything you tell me. Anything, divine creature."

As much as I enjoy being addressed that way, I prefer my name. "Call me Wrappa-Hamen!"

"Yes, divine creature, I mean, Wrappa-Hamen."

"I heard you tell Tashi about the woman at the Royal Tomb. I want you . . . hic . . . to take me there now."

"Oh, divine creature, I mean, Wrappa-Hamen, the Royal Tomb . . . hic . . . is guarded. You're asking me to spy!"

"The guards are only human. This is a divine . . . hic . . . matter. You have nothing to fear, I assure you."

Kush seems none too convinced. But he's in awe of me.

"All right, Wrappa-Hamen. I'll do it."

That said, he flops down on the bench and begins to snore. I shake him, I yell at him, but he's dead to the world. I'll just have to wait. But sleep is contagious, and Kush's snoring is hypnotic . . .

When I wake up, the light seeping through the reed mat covering the window is dimmer. At least two hours have gone by, and Kush is still asleep.

"Wake up!" I yell right in his ear.

"What the . . . ?" he says, coming out of his stupor.

"You useless drunk!"

I can see he's struggling to remember.

"All right, Wrappa-Hamen," he says after several seconds. "I'll go to the stable and fetch a donkey. Wait for me here."

He's almost through the door when he walks over to the jars of beer. Picking one up, he says, "We'll need this!"

Am I ever going to see him again?

Five minutes later, he puts his head through the door and tells me to come outside. I go on my fours. I don't want anyone else to know I'm a divine cat.

Out in the courtyard is a donkey with a basket containing the jar of beer tied to his sunken back. He's the saddest specimen of a donkey I've ever seen. He looks as if he's sleeping, and his head hangs down so low it's almost touching the ground.

And what's that noise? Snores? Worse?

"Is this the best you could do?" I ask.

"I'm afraid so," Kush says. "Tashi has taken the strongest donkeys. The others that are left are even worse than this one."

I'd hate to see the others. "How long will it take to get to the Royal Tomb?"

"It depends on Mut's mood," Kush says, pointing to the

donkey.

"Pick me up," I order, "and put me on Mut."

Kush lifts me and sets me down in front of the basket with the jar of beer. Mut brays. Is he saying I'm too fat?

Kush tries to plant himself behind the basket, and I feel Mut's back sink even lower. "Have you no pity for the poor animal? Get off immediately!"

Sighing, Kush gets down and tugs at the rope tied around Mut's neck until the donkey begins to move. After a few steps, Mut makes a sound my nose tells me isn't from his mouth.

When the village gatekeeper sees us approach, he starts to laugh. "Kush, have you mistaken your cat for your wife?"

"Shut up!"

"I'll kill him," Kush whispers under his breath.

As we pass through the gate, the gatekeeper puts a hand over his mouth to stifle more laughter. When a stifled laugh is finally emitted it's exceptionally loud, and after the gatekeeper closes the gate behind us, the volume of his laughter makes Mut's sensitive ears twitch.

He makes another noise, and this one doesn't come from his mouth either.

Looking north, I see big houses in the distance and ask Kush about them.

"Those are the houses of courtiers and rich merchants," he says.

"I'm new to the city. I've seen the quay and the southern part. I thought that was a rich area."

"Well, yes, it is. But the fat cats, sorry, I mean, the courtiers and rich merchants live in the northern suburbs as well as in the south."

As we proceed, the hills in front of us start to turn pink, and our shadows stretch longer and longer over the desert sand. Looking over my shoulder, I see the sun has begun its descent.

I shared hundreds of Egyptians sunsets with my beloved Pharaoh. How will I ever tear myself away from Egypt again?

"You haven't spoken for a while," Kush says. "What are you thinking?"

How could I possibly tell him? "If you must know, I've been

141

thinking how lucky you are to live in Egypt."

"Why don't you live here?"

"Let's say my heart lives here, my body somewhere else."

"But I see your body. It is here."

"Forget I said anything."

"I can't. You're a divine being. Whatever you say is unforgettable."

"If you don't forget it, I'll give you another demonstration of my powers. And I promise you'll feel this one even more!"

"I can't even remember what I'm supposed to forget."

"Good."

Except for the donkey's occasional braying, there's silence for a while.

Kush is the one who breaks it. "Do you see that gap in the cliffs?" he says, pointing to a dry river bed. "That's the Royal Wadi. It leads up to the Royal Tomb."

As we move closer, I see two guards patrolling the entrance to the Royal Wadi. One is tall, the other short. When we reach the entrance, they signal us to stop.

"Kush," the tall one asks, "isn't it late for you to be coming here?"

"The supplies were delivered late," Kush replies. "But at least there'll be beer this week. I'm bringing a jar to the guards at the Royal Tomb."

"What about us?" the short guard asks.

"Not all the beer has been delivered yet. More is coming tomorrow. I was told that the guards at the tomb were to get their beer first."

"Is that so?" the tall guard says. "Don't you think we should have a taste? Just to make sure it's fresh."

"Be my guest."

Kush takes the jar of beer from the basket on Mut's back and offers it to the guards. The tall one takes it, opens it, and drinks, spilling some of the beer on the sand.

Then he hands the jar to the short guard who takes his drink and says, "Ah, that's good beer. Too good for the guards at the tomb."

"You don't mean you're going to keep it?" asks Kush,

alarmed.

"Go on," the short guard says, winking at Kush. "Take it. It's not that good."

Kush takes the jar of beer back and puts it in the basket. Mut farts again and, holding their noses, the guards retreat a few steps.

"Was that your donkey?" the short one asks.

"No, the cat," Kush replies.

"Do us a favor," the tall one says. "Next time you come around, don't bring the cat." Before I know what's happening, he walks over to me and whacks me on the head with his baton.

"On your way!" he orders, and Kush resumes walking, pulling on the rope so Mut will follow.

"Why did you say I farted?!" I say, when we're out of earshot of the guards. "As if a cat's fart sounded like a blasting trumpet and smelled like a rotten carcass!"

"Didn't you tell me your body was somewhere else?" Kush says with a smirk. "Why would it matter to you that you got whacked?"

It seems Kush is a better philosopher than I am!

"How much longer to the Royal Tomb?" I ask him, changing the subject.

"With a good donkey, a good hour," he says. "With Mut, who knows?"

The scenery is boring, I'm still groggy from the beer, and I'm being swayed back and forth. Drifting off, I feel myself sliding down Mut's back and dig my claws in his fur.

And that's the last thing I do before leaving my fate in the hands of Kush and to the legs of Mut . . .

Chapter 22

"Wrappa-Hamen, wake up," Kush whispers, shaking me. "We're there."

I open my eyes. I'm slumped forward on Mut's back. I straighten up and look around. It's twilight, and we're in a desolate valley behind a large boulder.

"Where's the Royal Tomb?" I ask.

"Shush, not so loud," Kush whispers. "I don't want the guards to hear us."

"Aren't you going to give them their beer?"

"No, I'm keeping this jar for myself. They'll get their beer tomorrow just like the guards at the entrance to the Royal Wadi."

Kush has guts—guts that the guards at the tomb might remove if they ever find out he's been stealing their beer.

"Where's the Royal Tomb," I ask again.

"Look over the boulder."

I stand upright on Mut's back and peer over the top. There's a large opening in the ground in front of a rocky slope. Two guards are keeping watch.

"That's the entrance to the tomb?"

"Yes," Kush replies. "I'm leaving you here. I'll go no further."

I jump down. "You're leaving me here alone?!"

"You're a divine being. Don't tell me you're afraid."

"Of course not. I'm just wondering how I'll get back to the city."

"Let your divine mind come up with something. I'm not staying here!"

"All right. But before you go can we have some beer?"

Elena's voice tells me I shouldn't have any more, but the journey has made me thirsty.

"Good idea," Kush says, reaching for the jar in the basket on Mut's back. He takes the stopper out and lifts the jar to his mouth. I hear the gurgling sounds of the beer going down his throat.

"Well?" I say when he shows no sign of stopping.

"Sorry," he says, wiping his mouth with the back of his hand. "Cup your paws."

He pours beer into them, and I drink it all in one gulp. I offer my paws again. He pours more, and I drink it all, more slowly this time.

When he offers to pour more, I refuse. It isn't Elena's voice telling me to stop. The less I drink the more Kush does. Let him get so drunk that in the morning when he wakes up–the gods know where—he'll remember me as an hallucination.

"Drink the rest on your way home," I tell him. "You'll get thirsty."

"You are so smart, divine . . . Wrappa-Hamen."

"Just get going!"

Kush tries to bow, but falls head first and cries out. I help him turn over.

"Any blood?" he asks.

"No. But there will be if the guards heard you. And all of it will be yours. I can pretend to be an ordinary cat."

"I'll tell them you made me come here."

"Disappear," I say, exasperated, "before I call the guards myself."

I help Kush get up from the ground. Together we lift the beer jar and put it back in the basket on Mut's back. Then Kush picks up the rope dangling from Mut's neck and leads him away.

In place of a goodbye, Mut emits another of his fetid winds.

Soon they're out of sight and scent. Alone, I wonder how I'm going to solve the mystery of the woman who, dressed like a peasant, is allowed into the Royal Tomb.

Oh, you drunken cat—it's Elena's voice again—you should have thought about that instead of guzzling beer!

Yes, Elena, you're right. But I can't undo what's happened or leave and come back some other time. I have to act now!

Of course, the first thing to do is get inside the tomb. But I can't let the guards see me. I've already been whacked on the head by the guard at the entrance to the Royal Wadi. I'm not taking any chances with guards here. They haven't had a drop of beer in weeks and might take their frustrations out on an innocent passing cat, well, a passing cat.

I get down on all fours and peer around the side of the boulder. Where only moments ago there were only two guards, there are now four, two on each side of the entrance to the tomb.

Am I seeing double because of the beer?

I close my eyes for a few seconds. When I open them, there are still four.

Only one way to find out who's real and who isn't. I gather four pebbles from the ground and, standing upright, throw the first one at the guard leaning against the wall. He's real all right. He looks up, thinking he's been hit by a pebble falling from the hill above the wall. I throw a pebble at his double. He's real too. An illusion couldn't possibly curse that much.

Are the two guards on the other side of the entrance figments of my imagination?

I throw the third pebble, and hit one of them on the nose. Would an illusion be yelling like that? The fourth guard must be real too.

You see, Elena, I wasn't seeing double because of the beer.

I let the last pebble drop from my paw. But the three guards I've hit are walking toward the boulder. One of them is carrying a torch. Behind the boulder, I flatten myself on the ground as much as nature allows me.

When the guards come around the boulder, they can't see me even with the light from the torch. But they are very close. In fact, one of them is standing on my tail! The pain is excruciating, but I don't dare move.

"That was no falling pebble that hit me," one guard says. "It was thrown!"

"A nose as big as yours is a tempting target."

"But there's no one here," says the third guard. "Let's go back before we get in trouble for leaving our post."

"You forget our watch is over," says the guard with the big nose. "It's you and Mat who have to get back to your post."

You see, Elena, four guards because two are replacements. I was perfectly sober. Well, if not perfectly sober then, I am now. The pain in my tail has undone the effects of the beer.

When I hear the guards leave, I crawl to the edge of the boulder to make sure they're not coming back. One is walking back to the tomb. The other two are headed towards their camp. I stay where I am licking my aching tail when I catch a glimpse of another person walking toward the entrance to the tomb. I stop licking and take a good look.

It's a woman! I can't tell from the body, which is covered by in a long hooded woolen cloak, or from the face, which is almost fully obscured by a shawl, but from the small delicate feet. And on her feet are leather sandals embroidered with gold.

She's done a poor job of disguising herself as a peasant. What peasant wears gold embroidered sandals?

I get down on my belly and, staying close to the ground so the guards won't see me, crawl out from behind the boulder and toward the entrance to the tomb. When the woman approaches the two guards, they prostrate themselves before her. She passes them without taking notice of them and enters the tomb.

Before the guards can raise themselves, I get on my fours, race past them, and enter the tomb right behind her, the bottom of her robe tickling my nose. I back up a little so she won't detect my presence and, keeping a few steps behind, follow her.

The tomb is lit by oil lamps. Straight ahead of us is a steep staircase with the sarcophagus slide running down middle. We descend to a sloping corridor. The woman proceeds carefully, keeping her free hand on the right wall for support. She's gone ten or fifteen steps when she stops and leans against the wall, breathing hard.

Is she ill?

A bat flies out of a doorway farther along the wall and soars over us, its screech startling me. If there's something I hate more than a rat, it's a bat, and where there's one, there are usually others.

The woman resumes walking, and we reach the end of the corridor. There's a small landing with another steep staircase. I'm exhausted and dread the prospect of descending more steps. Fortunately, she ignores the staircase, going through a doorway instead.

We enter a funerary chamber. Painted on the plastered walls are funerary scenes and scenes of the royal family making an offering to the god Aten in a temple. The woman goes through a passageway to a room containing furniture that will be needed in the afterlife. From there, I follow her into another chamber, the smallest of the three.

It's the burial chamber. The large sarcophagus in the center almost fills it. The woman walks over to the head of the sarcophagus, throws herself upon it, and starts to moan.

I back out of the doorway, hide behind the wall, then peer around the corner to observe her. Because of the shawl, I still can't see her face. After a few moments, her moaning turns into faint crying.

Who is she grieving over? Whose body is in the sarcophagus?

Her crying abruptly ceases and she raises her head from the sarcophagus. I haven't moved or made a sound. She must sense my presence. I quickly pull my head in behind the wall.

"Who is there?" she asks, her voice husky from crying.

"A friend," I reply, without thinking.

"Show yourself."

Now I've done it! I wish the High Priest were here to advise me on what to say next. I don't know what else to do but tell the truth. "I can't."

"Then you are an enemy."

"I'm not."

"Are you disfigured?"

Her question gives me an idea. "Yes."

"I am above such things."

"But I'm not."

"Why do you intrude on my sorrow?"

"I didn't mean to. Whom do you mourn?"

"I mourn my beloved daughter Meketaten."

"I'm sorry for your loss."

"She loved it when I sang to her. I would sing to her now, but when she died, the songs I had in me died with her."

For the first time in my life, I have the urge to sing. I want to sing to her daughter!

After Elena played the opera *Norma* in New York, I listened to it on my own over and over again. The final scene never fails to thrill me. I remember every word of it! In the aria *"Qual cor tradisti"* Norma reproaches Pollione for betraying her and tells him death will now reunite them.

I sing Pollione's response to Norma. He professes his reborn love for her and asks her to forgive him . . .

"What is that divine song?" the woman asks when I finish.

"And the language? I've never heard anything so sublime."

"It's a love song. The language is Italian."

"Italian? I have heard many languages, but this is the most beautiful. Where do the Italian people live?"

"They live on a peninsula, in the middle of the Big Green."

"Have you been there?"

"No, but their songs are well known." It isn't the right time to tell her that the Italian cuisine is equally famous . . .

"I want to thank you for singing such a beautiful song to my beloved daughter."

"No need. It was my pleasure."

"Will I see you again? Or should I say, will we speak again?"

Before I can check myself, the word leaves my mouth. "Yes."

"Then, until we do, take this as a memento of our friendship."

I hear the ping of a small piece of metal hitting the floor on my side of the doorway. I look down to see a gold ring.

It'd be rude to refuse a gift! I stretch a forepaw, drag the ring to me with my claw, and put it in my mouth. It's small enough to keep inside my cheek.

I feel safe with this woman and want her to take me with her when she leaves the tomb at dawn. Wherever she lives, there'll be food and water.

"I wish to give you something in return," I tell her. "My cat. But I warn you. He likes his food and beer. Never let him go hungry or thirsty."

"Do not fear."

I go down on my fours, enter the chamber, walk over to her, and brush my head against her legs. The wool of her cloak is coarse but warm. She scoops me up and cradles me like a baby, holding my head tight between her neck and her shoulder.

"What is your cat's name?"

When no one answers, she says, "Your master is gone, and I don't know your name." She pauses for a moment. "I'll name you Tati. It was my daughter's nickname."

Gastone, Leopold, why not Tati? I purr, and she takes this to mean I approve.

The hand holding me tight loosens. She begins to stroke me. I turn to look up at her face.

A most beautiful face, the face of a queen. The face of Nefertiti . . .

Chapter 23

I wake from a troubled sleep, my head throbbing. If I never drink again, it'll be too soon. I'm no longer in Nefertiti's arms, but in a bed.

Nefertiti's?

I glance around. This is no ordinary bed, but a royal bed. And I'm not the only thing feline here. On either side of me is a masterfully carved lion head. The sides of the bed frame are carved in the form of lion bodies, the tails defiantly curved and on high. I feel at home in this bed, but I need to pee. I turn over and try to get up—

Too abruptly given the state I'm in! When I look down at the floor, the colored tiles are rearranging themselves in ever-changing patterns, just like the bits of colored glass in Elena's childhood kaleidoscope, which I played with for hours on end back in New York.

I lie back again, close my eyes, and, when the dizzy spell has passed, slide down to the footboard. It's inlaid with precious ivory and ebony. But it's only value to me is that I can use it to prop myself up.

This time I don't look down, but straight ahead. The mural in front of me leaves no doubt this is Nefertiti's chamber.

It's a family portrait, but no one is posing. It's like a photo taken without any of the subjects knowing, what Elena calls a candid photo. Nefertiti is with Pharaoh Akhenaten and their six daughters lounging in a columned hall.

The girls vary in age from infancy to adolescence. Nefertiti lies semi-reclined on cushions piled on the floor. Her back is propped up by more pillows set against a column. She's wearing a long pleated linen gown with elbow-length loose sleeves. Its red sash is loose, exposing her body. Her baby daughter sits on her lap. Two other daughters sit on cushions beside her. One sister lovingly caresses the other's chin.

Akhenaten is sitting on a stool. The three teenage daughters stand between him and their mother. Nefertiti's left arm encircles them, her hand resting on the waist of the one last in line. While her two sisters face their father, this daughter has turned her head to look at her baby sister. The baby's tiny hand is extended towards her, as if asking for the doll she holds. But instead of the coveted doll, her sister offers her a teasingly empty hand.

The little Pharaoh likes to grab my tail. His tiny hands are strong. If Nefertiti's baby daughter did get hold of the doll, there'd be no getting it away from her!

The mural celebrates Nefertiti's life with her family. But now it's a reminder of Meketaten's death. Which one is she? What happened to her sisters?

As if by magic, the curtains covering the entrance to the room are swiftly drawn. Nefertiti comes in wearing the same gown she does in the mural. For a moment, I think she's an apparition caused by my hangover. But then I see two women have entered behind her, one holding a small tray.

"Oh, Tati," Nefertiti says, picking me up, "I hope you slept well."

I didn't and I'm hungover!

Nefertiti takes me in her arms and carries me to a low pillowed stool by the left side of the bed. She sits and places me on her lap.

The woman with the tray sets it down on the small table in front of us. On the tray are combs, hair pins, and a bronze mirror. The hairdresser begins to use her tools on the wig Nefertiti is wearing. The wig is modeled on those worn by Nubian warriors. It hangs longer in the front, reaching the middle of her neck, and shorter in the back, barely reaching the nape.

Amazing how wearing a wig associated with men makes Nefertiti look even more feminine!

Looking down on me, she strokes my head. Her fingers linger on my star, and I purr madly. When her fingers move to my scar, she leans forward to take a closer look. "Ah," she whispers, "my little warrior. Is your master a warrior too? Was he disfigured in battle?"

At being called a warrior, I purr not just madly but ecstatically!

Nefertiti's breath smells of honey and cinnamon. I look up at her face. In the semi-darkness in Bath and in the Royal Tomb last night, I didn't notice the fine lines marking it. Her lips and cheeks show a hint of reddish brown make up. Her eyes are heavily defined by black kohl, emphasizing their beauty and making her look mysterious.

I let my eyes move downward. Her bejeweled broad collar reaches to the top of her breasts. Her breathing animates the rows of flowers, fruit, leaves, and petals made of precious jewels. So close to her, I'm aware of the maturity of the body under the gown. The slightly fallen breasts and belly.

I feel her shiver. A tear drop falls on my head, and I look up to see another tear about to slide off her cheek. The hairdresser is standing behind her and does not notice.

Nefertiti is staring at something in front of her. I know what she's looking at.

"Stop fussing about," she says sternly. "And hand me the mirror."

The hairdresser takes the mirror from the tray and holds it for Nefertiti to look into, moving it as she turns from left to right. Barely glancing into it, she nods her head. The mirror is taken away and the hairdresser is dismissed.

The other woman who came in with Nefertiti has been standing still as a statue by her side. A lady-in-waiting no doubt, waiting patiently. She's been smiling at me. The same smile the young merchant's wife gave me when I licked the honey off her finger. Her sheath dress falls from just below her ample breasts. The wide shoulder straps holding it up barely cover them.

Wonderful pillows, like Kaya's . . .

"Tia, do you think Djhutmose has waited long enough?" Nefertiti asks her.

Who's Djhutmose?

"He deserves to squirm a bit longer," Tia answers.

What has he done?

Nefertiti laughs, almost in self-mockery. "That might very well be, but nevertheless we should go. It's time to teach Djhutmose a lesson."

Lesson?

Tia takes me off Nefertiti's lap and sets me on the floor. Nefertiti rises and walks toward the doorway. Tia and I follow. As if by magic, the curtains are again swiftly drawn as Nefertiti

153

approaches them. Once through the doorway, I see the magic is the work of two young girls, one standing on either side of the curtains.

We walk across a corridor and enter another room. My head is still throbbing so I try not to move it and look only at what's directly in front of me.

Starting at the threshold and going straight across the floor is a pathway. Its borders are formed by a series of colored stripes. It's covered with figures of foreign men, one after the other, separated by three war bows. Each figure is upside down in relation to the one before.

There were similar pathways in my Pharaoh's palace. The design is a symbol of Egypt's enemies. To walk on the pathway is to trample on them.

Egypt's enemies are my enemies. I'd like to pee on them!

Actually, I'd better try not to think about peeing. I've had the urge to pee since I woke up and I don't want to have an accident.

"It will be such fun to teach Djhutmose a lesson," Nefertiti says.

"Yes," Tia says. "I can't wait to see his reaction."

The more I hear of Djhutmose, the happier I am not to be him.

Outlined in black and set against a bright yellow background, the figures beneath me are beginning to look as if they could reach up out of the floor and grab me.

Unsettled, I step off the pathway onto the marsh that's painted on the rest of the floor. As I walk around, I see that it abounds with life. Kingfishers, ducks, and other fowl fly above it. Calves leap through it. Red poppies and blue cornflowers grow everywhere. Against the marsh's earthy colors they seem bright flames and shining sapphires . . .

Exploring the marsh was just the distraction I needed!

Feeling more myself, I look for Nefertiti and Tia. They've walked to the end of the pathway to a colorful stone platform set against the wall. On the platform a throne awaits. Followed by Tia, Nefertiti climbs the steps of the ramp set in the middle of the platform and takes her place on the throne. Tia stands in front of the platform beside a tall lathed table on which an object has been

154

placed covered with a piece of linen.

What could it be?

I move as close to the platform as I dare, then sit. Painted around its base and on each side of the ramp is a row of more foreigners. These aren't Egypt's enemies, but her friends and allies. Each of the foreigners is kneeling in front of a small stand holding a basket of offerings. They're paying homage, their arms up in sign of respect.

I recall such scenes from the year I spent with my Pharaoh. Sometimes he was presented with an offering of food and would give me a taste of the foreign delicacies . . .

Each row of foreigners is set between a simple white skirt at the bottom and a molded cornice at the top. The edges of the cornice are striped with poppy red, lapis blue, emerald green, and brilliant white. I'm so happy that Bastet's gift enables me to enjoy such vivid colors.

There's so much more to feast my eyes on, like the murals and the decorated ceiling. But I turn my attention to Nefertiti, more splendid than any artistic creation.

She claps once, and a man, bowing low from the waist, comes through a doorway in the left wall.

"Stand up straight, Djhutmose," she says when he stops before her.

He obeys, keeping his eyes cast down. He's middle-aged, and has angular features that contrast with his round, copious belly, and wears a sleeveless linen tunic and a pair of leather sandals. His pot belly and attire leave little doubt he's well-to-do—a fat cat, if I may.

"Look up, Djhutmose," Nefertiti commands him.

He raises his eyes, studies his surroundings, and begins to stare at the covered object on the table.

"You have been summoned to explain that to me," Nefertiti says, pointing. "Go ahead. Uncover it."

Djhutmose approaches the table hesitantly and, with a trembling hand, removes the linen cover. His mouth opens. He's flabbergasted.

So am I! He's uncovered Nefertiti's famous bust. As in the future, its left eye is missing.

155

"I . . . I . . . ," Djhutmose says.

"Quiet," Tia admonishes. "How dare you speak!"

"That was delivered yesterday," Nefertiti says. "You had told me this would be the best work you had ever done. Is there an unspoken message in the missing eye? Are you trying to tell me I am blind in someway? Speak!"

Beads of sweat begin to appear on Djhutmose's forehead. "Queen Ankhkheprure Nefernefruaten, there . . . there were two eyes—"

"Silence!" Nefertiti commands. "Take that horrible thing back to your shop and never, never bring it back."

She stands, passes Djhutmose without giving him a glance, and walks down the ramp. Tia, right behind her, gives him a dirty look before following her queen out of the room.

I'm alone with Djhutmose, who's studying the bust, looking even more dumbfounded than before. When I get up to follow Nefertiti and Tia, he notices me for the first time. I don't like his expression. It's the look of a man who would kick a cat out of frustration. Having no intention of giving him the chance, I make a hasty retreat.

Outside in the corridor, I hear peals of laughter resonating from somewhere in the palace. I follow the sound, and it takes me back to Nefertiti's bedchamber. She and Tia are laughing. But Nefertiti's laughter is forced, and her right hand is clenched in a fist.

"My queen," Tia asks. "do I have your permission to go to the Great Palace? I can't wait to tell the girls in the harem about Djhutmose."

"You may, Tia. I will be resting a while. I am very tired after last night."

"Oh, my queen, please don't go back to the tomb again."

Nefertiti dismisses Tia's concern with a wave of her hand. Tia knows better than to insist.

"Take Tati with you," Nefertiti says. "Make sure he is fed."

"I will, my queen."

All this is music to my ears. I'll be listening to gossip while being fed. What more could I ask for?

Actually, I could do with a sandbox. I haven't relieved myself since last night, and my bladder is about to explode.

Tia picks me up. As she's retreating backwards from the room, I hear something fall on the floor. Nefertiti's left hand is open at her side, and a tiny object shines at her feet.

An almond-shaped crystal eye.

Chapter 24

I'm in Tia's arms being carried across a bridge. I picture the High Priest's archaeological map of Akhenaten to get my bearings. We're crossing the Royal Bridge. Tia and I have left the King's House on the eastern side of the bridge and are headed for the Great Palace, which can be entered from it.

The roof of the Royal bridge is held up by thin pillars set far apart on the parapets. I'm facing Tia's ample breasts, but if I turn my head I can see over the parapets down to the Royal Road. It's the widest road I've ever seen, more than a hundred feet. In my Pharaoh's time there'd be nothing to match it.

To the north it stretches as far as the eye can see. To the south it stops past the King's House by the Small Aten Temple.

The view from the bridge is breathtaking. Palaces, temples, villas, all gleaming in the sunlight. So too the twin towers of the pylons. Gateways to the temples and the palaces. Anchored to each tower is a pair of wooden flagpoles reaching from the base to well above the top.

The flagpoles have always been my favorite sight. They make me think of giant sentinels. Always standing at attention, never able to leave their post.

The flags are drooping till a northernly wind suddenly makes the material flap and flutter like the mighty wings of the vulture, the bird form taken by the goddess Nekhebet, protector of Upper Egypt.

I enjoyed the protection those wings promise during my year at court with my Pharaoh. How I miss it now! And how I miss Egypt's never-ending beauty and natural treasures—the clear blue daytime sky where the sun reigns supreme, the night sky where millions of stars shine like bright eyes, the recurring miracle of the Nile inundation. In losing my Pharaoh and then Egypt herself, I twice lost paradise—

"Oh, you are a hefty cat," Tia says. "There has to be a better way to carry you!"

She turns me around. I now face the far side of the Royal Bridge and catch glimpses of the open interior of the Great Palace, a complex of houses and courts. One large court is lined with colossal statues of the king and queen. But Nefertiti in life is far more majestic than her gigantic sculpted image—

I feel myself slipping from Tia's arms!

"I almost dropped you," she says, stopping. She lifts me back up and turns me around again, this time gripping me tighter. "That's better."

Now my face is stuck between Tia's breasts, and I can't see. But I'm still aware of her progress. When I'm bounced she's moving in a straight line, when I'm jolted she's going up or down steps, and when I'm bumped by one of her breasts she's turning a corner. And when I hear her being saluted by strong manly voices, she's going through a guarded gate.

Music is being played somewhere in the Great Palace, and with each of Tia's steps we get closer to it. A few moments later she stops and loosens her tight grip on me. I raise my face from between her breasts, look around, and literally face the music.

It's coming from a group of girls. They're under a columned portico that faces an open court with a sunken garden in the middle.

Three of them are musicians. One is playing a large lute, another a double oboe, and the last a tambourine. Three other girls are clapping in rhythm. Two more are dancing around the columns.

"Lady Tia, Lady Tia," cry the clappers and the dancers, stopping as the musicians keep on playing.

In an instant they encircle her. They're in their teens, but old enough to wear wigs. And such pretty wigs they are—adorned with faience beads and colorful ribbons.

Their expensive jewelry leaves no doubt they're the daughters of noble families or high officials. Because of their lofty parentage, they have the privilege of living at court.

The two dancers look like sisters. They wear only a thong and are panting. Their pyramid-shaped breasts are at the level of my eyes, advancing and retreating.

The three girls who were clapping resemble neither the dancers nor one another. One is thin, one quite plump, the other a mixture of the first two—thin on top, large at the bottom—what Elena would call pear-shaped. All three wear the same sleeveless tunic-like dress of transparent linen. Their bodies are less exposed than the dancers', but only slightly.

All five girls talk at the same time.

"I'm so happy to see you, Lady Tia."

"Come and sit with me."

"Have something to eat with us."

"Quiet down girls," Tia says, and to the musicians who are still playing, "Take a break now."

They quickly obey, leaving the portico.

"I have some good gossip to relate," Tia announces.

The girls draw closer to her, like iron to a magnet.

"But first, Nofret and Tetisheri," Tia says to the dancers, "get dressed. Look at you, sweaty from dancing. You'll catch a death."

"Go on Tetisheri," says Nofret, nudging her. "Get the gowns."

"Why do I always have to fetch things?"

"Because you're the youngest here, and you need to learn obedience."

Nofret is a bully, but Tetisheri is a mule. In the end, it's Nofret who fetches their gowns from the floor by the stools.

"What's the cat's name, Lady Tia?" the thin clapper asks, petting me on the head.

"His name is Tati, my dear Werel."

"He's fat," the pear-shaped clapper says. "I bet he eats a lot."

Well, I never!

"I assume he does, my dear Reonet. That reminds me. He needs to be fed."

"He could skip a meal or two if you ask me," the plump clapper says.

No one asked you!

"Look who's talking," says Werel. "You, Heket, could skip a meal or two, or three."

Heket replies by sticking her tongue out. Then she starts to pet me, but her touch is too rough for my liking. I free myself from Tia's strong hold, jump down, and go into the sunken garden.

Some of the girls want to chase me, but Tia stops them. "Leave the poor beast alone. You've overwhelmed him."

In the garden, hidden by the foliage, I can finally do what I've wanted to do since I woke up. Pee and pee to my heart's content!

When I finish, I race back, afraid to miss anything. Everyone

160

is sitting on a stool now, the girls in a semicircle facing Tia. Near the stools are small stands with baskets full of delicacies.

I take a roasted goose leg and sit on the floor. The goose leg is even more delicious than I imagined it would be. I'm close enough to hear what's being said, but far enough to be safe from Heket's rough touch.

"Be quiet," says Tia, giving the girls a stern look. "Don't interrupt as you usually do. Now, you know my sweetheart works in sculptor Djhutmose's workshop."

All five girls nod.

"Well, Djhutmose is an insufferable pain in the butt. He pushes his workers around and never appreciates their efforts, not even my sweetheart's."

"He's like that cow, our writing teacher," Werel says. "She never gives us her approval, no matter how well we do."

"You should hear how she reprimands us if we're five minutes late for a lesson," Heket says.

A dirty look from Tia stops the others from adding their own opinions of the writing teacher.

"Where was I?" she asks.

"You were telling us Djhutmose doesn't appreciate his workers," Nofret says.

"Yes, yes," Tia says, slapping her forehead. "Well, Djhutmose sculpted a limestone bust of the queen. Yesterday it was delivered to her, and she told me me it was the best work the man had ever done. But then I told her how badly he treated his the workers, and she decided to teach him a lesson."

"What did the queen do?" Tetisheri asks excitedly.

"Shhhh," Nofret says. "Let Tia speak."

"The queen asked me to have my sweetheart come over and remove an eye from the bust."

"What?!!!" the girls cry out in unison.

Forgetting myself, I chime in. No one notices, but realizing how close I came to giving myself away, I almost choke on a morsel of roasted goose.

"At the queen's instruction," Tia continues, "my sweetheart removed the eye very carefully, then all traces of glue to make it look as if the eye had never been put in."

161

"But why?" the girls cry out.

My question too, but I keep it to myself.

"To humiliate Djhutmose the way he humiliates his workers, of course," Tia replies.

Indeed! That's what Nefertiti meant when she said it was time to teach him a lesson.

Tia tells the girls what happened this morning in the reception room. She stresses how Djhutmose sweated and how dumbfounded he looked. The girls respond with ohs, ahs, and laughter. But I'm quite somber. The look Djhutmose gave me wasn't one of frustration, but of murderous intent.

To console myself, I walk over to the baskets of food, help myself to a pastry, and gulp it down before returning to my spot.

"I would have given my new wig to have been there to see it all," Werel says.

"Me too," the others say in unison.

"It is the queen's intention," Tia says, "to let some time go by before the eye is found, as it were."

"Oh, the queen is so good," Reonet says.

"So good, so good," the rest chime in.

Indeed she is. But how is it that thousands of years later the left eye is still missing?

"I must be going now, girls," Tia says. "I'll come back later to pick up Tati."

When she leaves, the girls discuss which game to play.

"Let's play Hide and Seek," Tetisheri says. "We haven't played that in a long time."

"Hide and Seek it is," Werel says, putting off any other suggestion.

I used to play Hide and Seek with my Pharaoh. It was easy for me to find him because of his distinctive odor, fresh lotus blossoms . . .

"But I'm not going to be 'it,'" Tetisheri insists.

"We'll do it by process of elimination. Gather around."

Werel points first at herself, then at Reonet, Heket, Nofret and Tetisheri as she chants, "One, two, three, four, five blow a whistle if you're a cow."

The last word falls on Heket. She's out. Werel counts again,

162

and she's the next one out. Reonet takes over, and she's out. It's Nofret's turn next, and she's also eliminated.

"Cheats, cheats," Tetisheri yells. "You're all cheats!"

"If it'll make you shut up," Nofret says to her sister, "I'll be 'it.'"

She walks to the back of the portico, and the other girls follow. "I'll sing 'Tonight my love will come,'" she tells them, "while you go and hide." She faces the wall, puts her forearm up, and leans forward, covering her eyes.

At the first word of the song, the girls take off. Werel and Reonet run into the garden and disappear, one to the left, one to the right. Tetisheri seems not to know where to go, then also heads for the garden. She hides behind a plank of wood set against the right wall, most likely part of some work in progress. Heket enters the doorway in the middle of the wall Nofret is leaning against.

Dying of thirst, I help myself to the pomegranate juice left by one of the girls. It turns out to be wine, but that doesn't stop me from drinking all of it.

". . . and his kisses will tell if his love is true," Nofret sings, ending her song. "Ready or not, here I come," she yells, leaving the wall and running into garden.

I begin to feel warm from the wine and long for a cooler place. I go through the same doorway as Heket, find myself in a pillared cross hall, and walk along a pathway, trampling on Egypt's enemies as I did in the King's House.

On either side of the pathway, just as in the King's House, lies a painted marsh. But here each marsh has a pool in the middle. Fish and ducks are swimming lazily around blue and pink lotuses.

Putting my forepaws in water will cool me off, and—who knows?—I might catch a fish while I'm at it! I step off the pathway and quickly cross one of the marshes to the pool. I lean over the edge and put my forepaws in the water.

Oops! The pool is just another piece of painted floor.

But the ripples in the water? I walk out onto the pool to have a closer look. Ah, just zigzags of white paint! Was it artistic skill or the effects of wine that fooled me? Both? In any event, treading on the pool has made me feel cooler.

Heading back to the pathway, I cross the marsh again, slowly this time, so I can appreciate its artistic wonders. Birds, dragonflies, and butterflies are flying about. The occasional calf leaps through the thick vegetation. Tall stalks of papyrus are swaying in the wind.

Is that a breeze I feel on my face?

Rising from the marsh along each length of the pool is a row of four stone columns. I look up. The shafts are covered with fluted emerald-green faience tiles. They look like giant flower stalks. Each capital is carved in the shape of a blooming lotus and painted in natural colors with touches of gold in the grooves. These enormous flowers reach the sky—a lapis-blue ceiling with a variety of birds flying in all directions . . .

I'm brought out of my trance by Nofret's distant voice. "Where are you, girls? I'm going to get you."

From ahead comes stifled laughter. Heket's?

The pathway with Egypt's enemies leads toward the source of the laughter. I get back on it, and it takes me into a square hall, also with columns. The pathway is crossed by another, dividing the hall into four parts, each with two rows of two columns. The floor in each part has a painted pool just like those in the cross hall.

I stop at the intersection of the pathways and sniff the air for traces of Heket. But all I smell is the wine on my breath and the various perfumes from the girls' hands.

Directly in front of me, set in the back wall at the end of the pathway, is a dais with a throne. I'm drowsy from the wine and consider going over to lie on it. I don't think Nefertiti would mind.

But again I hear stifled laughter. This time it's coming from my left. I turn onto the pathway leading to it and walk through an entrance to another pillared hall. The columns are decorated to look like palm trees. The floor, as in the other halls, is covered with painted pools and marshes.

I see a lion attacking a calf. So much for idyllic nature!

Someone springs at me from behind a column and scoops me up in her arms. Heket! She's hot, sweaty, and giggling.

"Now where is that chest?" she says, tightening her grip as she carries me down the corridor just outside the hall and into a small room with two big chests. She raises the lid on one of them.

There's clothing in it. Is this a robing room for the royals?

164

Before I realize what she intends to do, Heket climbs into the chest, taking me with her, and pulls the lid down. Her heart is beating fast and loud.

I don't like enclosed spaces. I especially don't like this one, sharing it as I am with an excitable girl who's holding me tightly.

When I get accustomed to the darkness, I see Heket's eyes. Behind her is another pair of eyes, much smaller and staring coldly. I'd like to be mistaken, but they're the beady eyes of a mouse.

I'm one of those rare cats who's afraid of mice. It's a fear I share with humans, especially females, and what happens next can only be described as "hysteria." I cry out, the mouse squeaks, and Heket screams at the top of her lungs.

I struggle to free myself from her grip. She lets go, then pushes the lid up and jumps out of the chest. I'd follow, but I'm entangled in some of the clothing. The lid comes down. I try to push it back up, but it's too heavy. I hear Heket's screams getting fainter and fainter.

The mouse and I stare at each other for a long, long time. Then he suddenly disappears. I crawl over, push aside the clothing, and see a hole in the side of the chest. A hole big enough for a mouse, but not a cat.

I put my mouth to the hole and meow loudly. Someone is bound to hear me and come to my rescue . . .

Chapter 25

Hours later no one has come. Abandoning hope, I curl up and think of Elena and the little Pharaoh. I miss them so much! And the High Priest too. Where is he? I wish he could help me.

I also think of Djhutmose. I blame him for my predicament. If he weren't a bastard, Nefertiti wouldn't have concocted her scheme, and Tia wouldn't have come here to tell the girls. And if she hadn't come, neither would I. If I survive this, I promise you, Djhutmose, you'll never see that eye again—

The lid is lifted! I try to stand up, but become entangled in clothing. I can't see because there's a garment over my head.

"A ghost!" a woman cries at the top of her lungs.

I bolt out of the chest, taking some of the clothing with me. I couldn't run faster if death were after me. I free myself of the garment covering my head. It's nightfall. The sky is already swept with stars. I reach the sunken garden where I peed earlier. The plank of wood is still here. I climb up the plank and find myself on a roof.

I see the roofs of other structures in the Great Palace and the wall enclosing them, and, looking down, the Royal Road. Heading north walks a lone figure. The distinctive Nubian wig and the long woolen peasant's cloak leave no doubt it's Nefertiti.

She's walking in the direction of the Great Temple. Is that her destination?

Keeping her in sight, I walk along the edge of the roof till I reach a gap separating it from the roof of the next building. The gap is too wide for me to leap over. But I easily jump over to the top of the outer wall of the Great Palace. Walking along it, I continue to follow Nefertiti till she reaches the Great Temple. It's on the opposite side of the Royal Road, and I lose sight of her when she enters the gateway.

I want to get down from the wall, cross the Royal Road, and enter the gateway myself. But the wall is too high for me to reach the ground safely.

I have to see where Nefertiti is going!

I continue walking till I reach the north wall of the Great Palace. In the middle of the wall I see the twin towers and the flagpoles of a pylon.

If I could climb up a flagpole, I might be able to look down into the Great Temple and spot Nefertiti. But I have to climb to the top of the tower to reach the flagpole.

I walk along the wall to the tower and look up. It's quite a climb!

Fortunately, the stone is pitted with small holes. It's tough going, but I manage to pull myself up the tower by catching my claws in them. I jump onto the flagpole, dig my claws into the precious cedar wood, and climb to the top.

I was right. From this height, I can look down into the Great Temple.

It's a vast walled enclosure containing a roofless long temple in the front and in the back a separate walled yard with a sanctuary. Inside the long temple and along the outside of its south wall are hundreds of small brick altars to hold offerings to the god Aten. A hundred or so more are in the sanctuary. On some of the altars the offerings remain. I see flowers and burning incense. But the food offerings have been removed to be eaten by the priests—

The yelps of jackals break the silence. I look up toward the hills above the city. But the jackals are too far away to be seen.

I hear another sound. This one is pleasant and soothing. It's the sound of the flowing Nile. I look down at the river. The reflection of the stars on its surface makes it seem a piece of fallen sky. Egypt, forever casting spells on men and cats alike.

But I must not forget about Nefertiti!

Returning my gaze to the long temple, I see her pass the small brick altars outside the long temple and disappear behind it. She reappears on the pathway that runs in a straight line from the rear of the temple to the sanctuary.

Of course, she's headed for the sanctuary!

Nefertiti enters the gate to the walled yard surrounding the sanctuary and walks toward the pylon dividing it into two courts. She crosses the first court, but when she reaches the pylon, she falters, stops, and leans against the wall of the right tower.

Is she ill or just resting?

She brings her right arm up against the wall and rests her head against it. In her right hand is a long shiny object. Abruptly, she moves away from the wall, goes through the pylon into the second court, and follows the pathway to its end. She's in front of a stepped platform where the high altar rests.

Fearing the worst, I race down the flagpole, cut diagonally across the field fronting both the Great Palace and the Great Temple, and cross the Royal Road.

"Never seen a cat so fat run so fast!" says a guard as I pass through the pylon of the Great Temple. "Is death chasing him?"

If I'm right, I'm chasing death!

I stop once to catch my breath, midway between the long temple and the sanctuary. I resume running and don't stop again till I've climbed the steps to the high altar where Nefertiti is now standing.

Her head is tilted back. Her right hand is above her chest and holds a dagger. She must hear me panting loudly, but she doesn't look at me. Her eyes are on the sky. Her lips are moving as if she were talking, but there's no sound. She's in a trance, like a somnambulist.

I stand upright, intending to reach for the dagger—

Suddenly, I start to cough the way I do when I'm about to vomit a fur ball!

Nefertiti's right hand is slowly bringing the dagger down to her chest. But I'm gagging and can do nothing. The dagger is but inches from her chest when I feel the fur ball coming up, cough violently, and spit it out.

It hits the blade of the dagger, and I hear the sound of metal striking metal. A shiny object falls at Nefertiti's feet.

For the love of the gods! It's the ring she gave my master, I mean, me in exchange for singing for her in the Royal Tomb. I'd forgotten all about it. I must've swallowed it when I was asleep.

Nefertiti drops the knife. As she starts to look around, I get down from the platform and hide behind one of the small altars on either side of it. From here, I can still see her, and she seems frightened. She looks down, sees the ring and the dagger, and stares at them, puzzled.

"Where are you?" she asks, looking around. "You have not told me your name."

"My name is Pollione," I say, using the name of the Roman

proconsul who betrayed Norma—concealing my identity from Nefertiti is a form of betrayal.

"Pollione," she says. "What a strange, but wonderful name. Is it Italian like the song you sang to me last night?"

"Yes."

"Pollione, how is it I am here?"

"You were sleepwalking."

"And the dagger?"

"Sit, and I'll tell you."

Nefertiti sits on the platform, her knees to her chest, her arms wrapped around her legs.

When I describe what I've seen, she shivers. "It is the end, the end," she whispers.

"The end of what?"

"Of a dream."

I'm about to ask her what she means when she continues.

"Oh, Aten, so much has been sacrificed in your name. The old temples were closed. We told our people to abjure all other gods. We did not ask them. We told them. We erased the names of the other gods from ancient stone in a futile attempt to erase their memory from our people's hearts. But the people remember. They remember and mourn. Silence and fear pervade our land. Many honor the old gods in secrecy, fearful of their neighbors reporting them."

She pauses, sighing. I wish I could go to her and try to comfort her.

"And now I reap the rotten fruit of that tyranny. Akhenaten's love for me has turned to hatred. My daughters, the ones death spared, are lost to me. He would not even let me visit my dear Meketaten's tomb, because she was the one who never faltered in her love for me. I took to going there in disguise, but he found out. Yesterday, he decreed her burial chamber be sealed. Last night was the last time I could be with my daughter . . . Such is his hatred for me."

"Hatred? But just yesterday I saw you and the king riding together in your chariot."

"It was only for the sake of appearances, my dear Pollione."

"But why does he hate you?"

"I try to make him see what we have done to our people."

"You are co-regent. Can't you help Egypt yourself?"

"I do what I can. But I must be careful. The country is riddled with Akhenaten's spies. I am not afraid for my life—indeed, as you have just witnessed, I want to end it—but I fear his revenge on those I try to help."

"How sad."

Nefertiti raises her right hand and points to the sky. "I have but one wish," she says, "to join the 'Indestructibles.'" The stars that never fall below the horizon. For the ancient Egyptians a symbol of immortality.

Poor Nefertiti, she will have immortality, but not the kind she seeks.

"But with you gone Egypt would lose its only hope."

"Oh, Pollione, what you say is true. During the day I am able to keep despair at bay, but at night . . . my heart controls me."

I have human powers, but I can't offer her a human embrace. Oh, my accursed feline body!

"I am tired, Pollione," Nefertiti says, lying down on the altar. "Will you sing what you sang for me last night?"

With the little strength I have left after the run, I again sing Pollione's response to Norma in the sad aria *"Qual cor tradisti."* By the time I finish, she's asleep.

I leave my hiding place and approach her. She lies on her back, her left shoulder exposed, and I pull on her robe to cover it. She sighs. I lie at her feet, like the dog on a medieval knight's tomb. I leave her side and go back into hiding when I feel sleep is about to overcome me . . .

I dream of Nefertiti. We stand facing each other. I'm as tall as she is, if not taller. I hear faint notes of music, and as the music becomes louder, I recognize a Viennese waltz. I place my right paw on Nefertiti's back, and she places her left hand on my right shoulder. I take her right hand in my paw, move it to the height of her shoulder, and we begin to waltz.

We turn faster and faster. First we're dancing inside Stonehenge, then on the pavement in front of the Royal Crescent. When we reach the entrance to her home, she's pulled away from me by an invisible force. The door behind her opens. She stretches her arms towards me, but I'm frozen in place, and she recedes into the vestibule.

"Don't go," I cry out. "Don't leave me!"

The door slams closed . . .

I feel the same despair I felt in the dream when I awake to discover that Nefertiti is gone. She's taken the dagger and the gold ring with her. I shake my head and hope I'm still dreaming.

No such luck! I'm fully awake and desperately alone.

It's just before dawn, and I hear the chanting of the priests welcoming the Aten to his new day. I make my way back to the King's House, hoping Nefertiti will be there.

With great trepidation I enter her bedchamber. I can barely contain my joy when I see her lying in her bed fast asleep. Stealthily, I crawl into her bed, curl up by her side, then lick her hand, the one I held in my paw as we danced. On her small finger she wears the gold ring.

"Tia could not find you, Tati," she says, awakening. "I was afraid you were lost."

If you only knew what that girl Heket did to me!

"Last night, I spoke with your master, Pollione. He has breathed new life into me."

And you, my queen, have breathed new life into me!

171

Chapter 26

When Nefertiti leaves to attend to her duties, I return to the quay and find the spot where the High Priest and I moored the boat.

It's gone! I spend the rest of the morning and a good part of the afternoon walking up and down the quay looking for it. But it's nowhere to be found.

Did the High Priest move it, or someone else? Was he on the boat when it was moved, or somewhere else? Most important, where is he now? I hate to admit it, but I need his guidance. According to the calendar in the King's House, today is the third day of the month of Epep. Which means we arrived here on the day prior to the beginning of Nefertiti's lost ten days, the last day of the month of Paoni, just as the High Priest had prayed for.

Poor High Priest, to think I doubted him!

I have seven days left to see what caused Nefertiti's amnesia! I'm assuming it was sudden. But how do I know something hasn't already happened in the last three days that will eventually cause her amnesia?

Confused and dejected, I walk back to the King's House, find a shadowy spot in the garden near the tool shed, and, exhausted, collapse into a dreamless sleep . . .

Much later, having attended to my bodily functions behind an acacia tree, I remember the glass eye—and my resolve to punish Djhutmose. I return to the bedchamber and look for the eye where I saw it fall.

It's not here. It's probably been found by a maid or swept somewhere by her broom. I search further and, sure enough, the eye looks back at me from under the bed. I take it in my mouth and return to the garden to bury it.

As I'm digging, I begin to have second thoughts about punishing Djhutmose. Tia told the girls that Nefertiti intended to return the eye to him when she felt he had suffered enough. It would ruin her plans if the eye went missing—

"What do you think this is, a toilet?" cries an man's angry voice.

I'm so startled I swallow the eye. Oh, for the love of the gods, that's going to be painful to pass!

I turn to face the man. A gardener who looks as angry as he sounds. As I make my retreat, I consider how lucky I am he didn't catch me behind the acacia tree doing exactly what he's accused me of.

In the days that follow I don't try to find the High Priest again. I have to believe he'll find me by finding Nefertiti as I did. He's sure to be searching for her urgently. Better I stay near Nefertiti. After all, my mission is to learn how she lost her memory.

I remain in the King's House resting, eating, and keeping a low profile just in case some excitable girl should get it into her head to scoop me up.

Today is the ninth day of Epep and still, as far as I know, nothing unusual has happened. But the time has not been completely uneventful. Two days ago Nefertiti sent a letter to her husband, Akhenaten, at the North Palace. I was by her side when she composed it. She was trying to reconcile with him.

Remembering what she'd said to me that night at the Great Temple, I doubted she'd succeed.

Early this morning she received his answer. The servants' whispers tell me her attempt at reconciliation has been met with scorn. It's now late morning, and despite Tia's many urgings, Nefertiti is still in bed. I'm with her, at her feet, afraid to leave her alone.

"Let me be," she tells Tia, who gives up and disappears behind the curtain over the entrance to the chamber.

I remain still with one eye on the queen. When she begins to sob, I crawl up to her chest. She's covered her face with her hands. I nudge her and she lowers them.

"Oh Tati," she whispers, cupping my face, her tear-filled eyes looking into mine. "Will I ever meet your master, Pollione, again?"

Not if I can help it, my queen!

"I must. He is the only ray of sunshine in an otherwise dark, dark existence."

Ah! I see . . .

I paw at her face gently, and she kisses my forehead. Like a crazed horse, my heart races at a frantic gallop. I lick her nose in

173

return. She laughs. She releases my head and I regain control of my heart's reins.

"Tia," she calls out.

Tia peeks from behind the curtain.

"I wish to bathe," Nefertiti says. "And have the chief steward send word to have the royal barge made ready. We are going for a cruise on the Nile."

Tia, looking relieved, comes in to help the queen out of bed. "Do you wish the cat to accompany you?"

"Of course."

"Well, carrying him in my arms has proven difficult. He's way too fat. I'll bring a basket for him."

"As you wish," says Nefertiti as she leaves the chamber with Tia following.

I'm so happy to see Nefertiti in a better mood that I don't dwell on Tia's uncalled-for remark about my weight. Besides, I've something more important to think about—how to fulfill Nefertiti's wish to meet Pollione again . . .

I have it!

On the table next to Nefertiti's cosmetic box is a small sheet of papyrus and a writing kit—a palette containing dry ink, reed pens, and a little jar. I pour a little water from a glass into the jar, dip the tip of a reed in it, brush the tip over the dry ink, and then, holding the reed firmly between my paws, I begin to compose . . .

When Nefertiti is ready we leave the King's House and head for the Great Palace. She leads the way, walking with the bearing of a lioness, followed by Tia, who carries me in an open cushioned basket.

Lifted by the wind, the bands of the red sash of Nefertiti's gown fly teasingly in front of my face. I can't help pawing at them, and Tia repeatedly pulls me back.

Behind us are the girls, all five. Bringing up the rear are four tall Nubian guards for our protection.

When we enter the Great Palace, we go in a straight line across an open court, then over a ramp into another court with at least two dozen stelae on each side. Though we're moving fast, I can see that the carvings on the stelae are scenes of the royal family worshiping their god Aten, the disk of the sun.

How laden with sadness Nefertiti's heart must be as she passes these reminders of happier times!

We walk across yet another court, then enter a courtyard. Nefertiti quickens her pace, the others follow suit, and before I know it we are exiting the courtyard through a stone gate and walking onto the royal quay.

Reaching into the Nile like welcoming giant arms and hands are two stone piers and their jetties. Moored at one of the jetties is the royal barge. The hull is covered with festive stripes of turquoise, red, and blue. The prow is painted with life-size portraits of the royal family. The huge carved blue lotus projecting from the stern looks like an actual giant flower.

We board the barge and proceed to the queen's cabin. The wooden pillars flanking the entrance have been carved to resemble trees bearing fruit of precious stones.

When we set sail, I sit in my cushioned basket and look out the windows on either side of the cabin. To the east, embraced by the golden cliffs behind it, stretches the city with its white stone temples and whitewashed brick palaces and houses. To the west are cultivated fields, a succession of shades of green punctuated by yellow stripes of ripening wheat.

What I don't see, I imagine—orchards bountiful with fragrant fruit and vineyards laden with clusters of grapes.

I hear the lapping of the Nile against the hull, the drumming of the wind on the sails, and the high-pitched chatter of gossiping girls mingled with the velvety sighs of the queen.

All this is more inebriating than any drink I've ever had! And if it weren't enough, the queen takes me onto her lap to scratch me under my chin, which I offer to her fingertips with all my being. The sounds I make, a crescendo of ecstatic purrs, drown out all the others.

Drunk with pleasure, I fall off the queen's lap! She, Tia, and the girls burst out laughing. I get up and, with tail on high, leave the cabin. They laugh even harder. Hearing giggling behind me, I turn around to see Heket trying to grab me and escape just in time.

I flee to the very tip of the giant lotus on the stern. As I sit keeping an eye on the silly girl, I'm stared at by the carved effigy of Nefertiti on the top of the rudder.

There's no escaping women, is there?

Nefertiti remains in good spirits throughout the day and in the evening before retiring she tells Tia that tomorrow she wishes to go Maru-Aten for a picnic. Tia is to inform the chief steward to have the chariots ready and to send word to Maru-Aten ahead of her arrival.

Unfortunately she tells Tia to bring the girls as well. Whatever games the girls will be playing at Maru-Aten, no matter how much fun their games might seem, I'm keeping my distance. Last time I joined in I ended up imprisoned in a chest.

It takes me a long while to fall asleep. I'm too excited thinking of the joy of exploring a new place and of the savoring the delicacies at the picnic . . .

Chapter 27

Maru-Aten turns out to be a lavish enclosed country estate with gleaming white temples and houses, luscious gardens, and, in the middle, a huge pond. At the far end of the estate, surrounded by a moat, is a man-made island just big enough for two small houses and a shut-ra, a roofless sun chapel.

We're having our picnic in the shut-ra. The tiled columns, the water plants painted on the walls, and even the beaded necklaces worn by my companions are the same shade of turquoise as the sky.

Has some celestial artist been at work here?

On a platform in the the center of the shut-ra, Nefertiti sits on a throne-like chair inlaid with ivory and ebony. I'm in my cushioned basket next to her. Tia and the five girls sit on pillows in a semicircle in front of the platform. Beside each picnicker is a low table that the servants have covered with plates of roasted quails, pickled cucumbers, honey cakes, duck eggs omelets, and stuffed figs.

I've been given a bowl, and Nefertiti has filled it with food from her table.

While eating, I look through the large square window over to the pond. Everyone in Maru-Aten is eating! Frogs leap from behind the thick foliage around the pond and stick their tongues out to catch flying insects. Kingfishers hover above the water, then suddenly dive, catching their prey in their beaks.

I enjoy the ducks especially. When one dips its head and neck in the water to get food, its ass pops up covered with droplets that shine in the bright sunlight, and the silly little tail points straight up to the sky.

Whenever possible, I sneak a few laps of wine from Nefertiti's goblet. The others are also drinking wine, and if one of them happens to place her goblet on the ground, I leave the comfort of my cushioned basket to sneak a few laps from it too.

Stuffed and a little drunk, I fall asleep in my basket to the lullaby created by the chatter of women, the humming of bees, the croaking of frogs, and the singing of birds . . .

When I awaken, there are three musicians outside the front

entrance to the shut-ra, sitting on the steps with their instruments, waiting to play.

Tia whispers in Nefertiti's ear, and the queen nods.

"Would you like to play musical statues?" Tia asks the girls.

"Oh, yes, yes!" they all chime in, getting up from their pillows and gathering around her.

"I'll be the game master of course," Tia says. "And the winner will receive this!" From behind her back, she takes a lovely beaded necklace and holds it up to the girls. "Get ready," she orders when their ohs and ahs die down.

Never heard of musical statues, but seeing the girls compete should be fun!

The girls spread out. "Go ahead," Tia calls to the the musicians. The music comes fast and loud. The girls are dancing frantically. "Stop the music!" Tia shouts suddenly.

The girls freeze, arms and legs extended. Tia goes around studying each of them. Heket bursts out laughing and loses her pose.

Typical of her. So excitable!

"You're out!" Tia orders.

Heket moves to the sidelines, and Tia has the music start again. When the four remaining girls are in the midst of their frantic dancing, she again tells the musicians to stop. Again the girls freeze. Again Tia goes around studying them.

Tetisheri, who has been left standing on one leg, begins to tremble so much she loses her pose. Tia calls her out, and she joins Heket.

In the next round, when the music stops and Nofret, Reonet and Werel freeze, Heket and Tetisheri make faces at them. They laugh and lose their poses.

"None of you took the game seriously," Tia says. "None of you deserve the necklace. I'll keep it for myself!"

I look up at Nefertiti, who's smiling sadly. These girls must remind her of her daughters. One has died, and she can no longer visit the tomb. The others she isn't allowed to see.

If I ever meet her husband, I'll scratch his face for making her suffer so!

Tia dismisses the musicians and proposes a game of hide and

seek. She'll be "it" and will count down from twenty before searching for them. She walks over to one of the columns, turns her back to the girls, and covers her eyes. When she begins to count, the girls take off.

Nofret, Tetisheri, Reonet and Werel all run out the front entrance and down the stairway. Nofret and Tetisheri each hide in one of the small buildings that flank the shut-ra. Reonet and Werel run past the buildings and over the bridge that connects the island to a temple and the rest of the estate.

Good riddance! But where is Heket?

I turn and see her leaning over me. How did she get onto the platform without my noticing?

Oh no, you don't!

I hiss at her. She jumps off the platform, runs out the back entrance to the shut-ra, and crosses the bridge leading to a walled flower garden.

"Here I come, girls!" shouts Tia when she finishes counting. She looks around, then goes out the front entrance to search for the girls.

Finally some quiet!

From her throne-like chair, Nefertiti is gazing at the pond as the declining sun tinges the water pink. I go back to lie in my cushioned basket next to her, unable to take my eyes off her beautiful somber face . . .

I become aware of the woman only as she climbs the last steps of the front stairway and enters the shut-ra.

If I'd been talking, I'd now become speechless. Though not quite as beautiful, the woman is a younger version of Nefertiti. She's even dressed in the same long pleated linen gown tied under her breasts by a sash. But her sash is blue rather than red.

She walks over the platform, steps up, and stands beside Nefertiti's chair. Only now is the queen aware of her daughter.

"Mother." Her tone would congeal a mother's blood!

"My dear Meritaten," Nefertiti says, either missing the chill in her daughter's voice or choosing to ignore, "I had hoped to see you here."

"And I had hoped you would never come here again!"

I'm stunned. Why such hatred?

"You are cruel," Nefertiti says.

"That is not what my father thinks of me."

"He has poisoned you against against me. I thought you, being the eldest, would understand that. Can you not see it?"

"What I see, Mother, is your betrayal of my father's ideals, my father's cause."

"Your father's cause has oppressed Egypt!"

"I will no longer listen to you. I will go to my father. When I come back tonight, I expect you to be gone."

With these words, Meritaten bows to Nefertiti and leaves the way she came.

If there was ever a time for Pollione to return, it's now!

I take the papyrus from under my pillow where I hid it yesterday. Keeping it between my teeth, I stretch up to Nefertiti's knees and offer it to her. Hesitant at first, she accepts it. I return to my basket as if nothing has happened, and she reads aloud,

No longer are the stars in the sky.
No longer is a man's heart his.
Thou, my queen, have captured all.

Nefertiti stands up, leaves the platform, and looks around, first toward the front stairway, then toward the back one.

When she returns moments later, she leans over to pat me on my head. "Oh, Tati, you are the best messenger in all Egypt."

She sits back down on her chair and closes her eyes. Holding the papyrus in her right hand over her heart, she falls asleep.

Suddenly, I sense someone else's presence in the shut-ra. I turn.

It's Heket!

I immediately discover why she's come out of hiding. With the speed of an arrow, she jumps on the platform, scoops me out of my basket, and, clutching me tight to her bosom, makes off with me out the back entrance.

Oh, for the love of the gods! It's my kidnapping in the Great Palace all over again!

We cross the bridge to the flower garden and enter a courtyard at the back of the garden. The courtyard contains a long row of interlocking T-shaped pools with large pillars between them.

Is Heket going to hide behind one of the pillars? Or in a water tank and drown me in the process?

I'm not going to stay around to find out. I hiss at her as ferociously as I can. She drops me and flees.

The wine I drank and the shock I just had have left me with an urge to pee. The flower garden seems like just the place. But I see what looks like a gardener. He has his back to me.

If he's anything like the gardener I encountered in the garden of the King's House, I'll be the victim of some unpleasantness if he sees me peeing! I'd better make it quick before he turns around. I look for a suitable spot in the flower beds.

How pretty the chamomile flowers look! Elena used to make herself chamomile tea before retiring at night. Sometimes she made some for the little Pharaoh to soothe his upset stomach.

I miss them both so much!

I pee under the chrysanthemums. When I leave the garden and return to the shut-ra, Nefertiti is gone. On her chair lies a memento of the day, the collar the girls made for her from the flowers and berries they picked in Maru-Aten before our picnic.

Sadly, the flowers have wilted and the berries dried.

Wafting on the air is the smell of incense. Aten is low on the horizon. As they do when he rises, the priests are again purifying the air in his temples with incense and making offerings of food and libations.

Indeed, Nefertiti must have gone to worship at one of the temples!

Mixed with the odor of incense is another familiar smell.

Why didn't I notice it before? Was it masked by perfumes worn by Nefertiti and the girls? Or is it because the northern wind has begun to blow and carries it to me?

I follow the smell back to the flower garden.

He's stooping from the weight of the gardener's yoke on his shoulders, a water pail hanging from each end.

"Gato-Hamen!" I call out, running over to him.

The High Priest straightens abruptly. The yoke slides down his back to the ground. The pails hit the ground hard, and the water splashes on me.

But I don't mind! I jump into his open arms and encircle his neck with my fore legs, tightly.

"What are you trying to do," he asks, "strangle me?!"

"I'm just so happy to see you."

"And I you."

Running his hands up and down my back, he comments on my weight gain and complains about the many days of starvation he endured before finding a gardener's job at Maru-Aten.

He is much thinner! If he weren't, I would've recognized him even from the back. But with his hands so close to my fat neck it might not be in my best interest to mention his weight loss.

"I took the job in the hope of meeting Nefertiti," he explains. "Knowing today was the tenth day of her amnesia, I had lost all hope. Then she arrived. Of course I did not know you were here as well . . . What the hell are you doing here?!"

"I thought you'd never ask." I describe my adventures from the moment I left him at the market to follow the merchant to the moment I gave Nefertiti my poem.

When I recite it, the High Priest smiles.

"What is it?"

"I did not tell you this in Bath, because it was a detail. When Nefertiti woke up on the eleventh of Epep she discovered a love poem she did not remember receiving. She recited it to me. It was your poem. You have always been part of her forgotten past."

"But I gave her the poem only today!"

"For the Nefertiti back in Bath, it was centuries ago. What is the present for you is the past for her, though forgotten—"

"Stop!" I cry, no longer feeling guilty over the High Priest's weight loss. "My head is spinning!"

His smile fades.

"What's wrong?"

"Whatever caused her amnesia will come to pass tonight. You must stay by her side to discover what it was. Then we can return to the future."

"Talking about returning to the future, where did you put the boat? I couldn't find it."

"It was too risky to leave it where it was. I kept moving it until I found the job here in Maru-Aten. It is nearby, just outside the walls, where I can keep an eye on it."

"I'm glad it's safe. But how did you move it here so far from the Nile?"

The High Priest doesn't answer.

"You used magic?"

"Er, well, yes. But at first it did not go smoothly. I ended up in another time."

"Where?"

"Ancient Rome. In a sewer . . . Please do not ask any more questions. Let us just say it was a low point in my life. Best forgotten."

The poor High Priest!

"You must go to Nefertiti now. Every moment is critical. I will be waiting to hear from you. During the day you can find me working in this garden or in gardens nearby. At night I will be in my quarters. My house is the first of the small houses to the left of the main entrance . . . You must go now!"

He puts me down and gives me a push. "Hurry!"

It pains me so to part from the High Priest again! Without looking back, I go to find Nefertiti.

I start at the temple beside the moat. All I find are priests performing their rituals at the altar where baskets of fruit and libations have been placed. One priest stoops to pet me. Though I'm on a urgent mission, I can't help circling his legs.

"Tati, Tati, where are you?" Tia calls from somewhere outside the temple.

I turn abruptly, almost tripping the priest, and follow the voice to the main gate of Maru-Aten. Tia and the girls are in couples waiting in chariots. Guards are at the rear. Nefertiti is standing next to Tia's chariot, cloaked in a wool cape. She's trembling, though there's hardly a breeze now.

Tia sees me and holds up my basket. "Come, Tati!"

I stop.

She gets out of the chariot and walks toward me.

I move back.

"Oh, let him stay here, Tia," Nefertiti says. "He will keep me company."

"My queen, are you sure you want me to go? I don't like to

leave you unattended."

"I wish to be alone. And there are plenty of women here to attend to my needs . . . Of course," she adds, seeing Tia's hurt expression, "none could serve me as well as you. Now go before Aten is swallowed up."

As soon as Tia and the girls leave in their chariots, Nefertiti has the guards bring a chariot for her. It's pulled by two magnificent stallions, their black coats glowing in the light of the torches at the sides of the gate.

Where is Nefertiti going? I don't have a good feeling about this.

As the chariot passes through the gate, I jump in. She seems not to have noticed. We ride south of Maru-Aten, fast and furious, her cape flapping in the wind like the mighty wings of a vulture. Riding on uneven ground, the chariot lurches and bounces. I fear the wheels will come off any minute.

A quarter of an hour later, we stop beneath the outermost edge of the cliff that hugs the city on its southern side. Nefertiti leaves the chariot and walks along a man-made path going up the craggy side of the cliff. I follow, keeping at a distance.

Twilight is almost over, but there's enough light left to guide her. Still she stumbles, and each time it happens, my heart skips a beat. She stops in front of a niche in the cliff where a stela has been carved out of the back wall.

What is this place? Sacred ground? Why has Nefertiti come here?

I stay in the shadows so she can't see me. She paces up and down, wringing her hands, looking repeatedly from left to right.

Appearing suddenly out of thin air is a man . . . Well, not entirely a man. His face is a long downward-curving snoot. Two asinine ears with flattened tips sprout from his head, and a tail sticks out from under his kilt.

I've seen his likeness painted on the walls of temples and tombs. It's Seth, the god of darkness and terror. He smells like stale urine.

He bows to the queen, his right arm raised in the henu gesture. It's a gesture of joy and respect, but his leering smile betrays his true feelings.

184

I'm shaking. My fur is standing up like steel bristles.

"Why have you summoned me here?" Nefertiti asks.

"My dear queen," Seth replies. "You prayed to me earlier today at Maru-Aten to make a bargain, and we did. All I have done is choose the time and the place to carry it out."

Seth's voice is mellow, but has a sting.

What bargain has she made with him? I should never have left her alone.

"Yes, but why here?"

"Call me a sentimental god. I thought what better place to carry out our bargain than where we first met. On this very spot, by that stela, you prayed to Aten to resurrect your dead daughter, your beloved Meketaten. He turned a deaf ear. Then you summoned me. But I had to decline. Resurrecting the dead is outside my expertise —"

"I still don't understand," Nefertiti says.

"Do not interrupt me! I am unforgiving. You and your husband had that stela carved and inscribed just before the building of Akhetaten, the city to honor Aten as the one and only god . . ."

His eyes turning a fiery red, Seth adds, "Monotheism, a huge mistake, may dear. It hurt a lot of gods. It pissed me off especially. So before we go through with our bargain I want you to put your hand on that stela and abjure your beloved god. It is a deal-breaker."

Bastard!

Nefertiti, without saying a word, moves to the back of the niche and puts her right hand on the stela. "I abjure the god Aten. I abjure all he stands for. I abjure the city that was built for him . . ."

The humiliation. My poor queen!

"Now come to me," Seth commands. Nefertiti obeys, stopping a few feet from him. "Close your eyes," he tells her, " and wish it away!"

Wish what away?

"My husband's love and my daughters' love are no more," Nefertiti says in a low monotone. "Nothing holds me here . . . Oh, Pollione, soon your disfigurement will be gone and you will no longer fear my gaze. Together we will leave this land, and in the days left to us we will find happiness . . ."

What does she mean? What have I done?

"Now!" Seth cries out.

Nefertiti has become luminous. Keeping the outline of her form, the pulsating white light slowly moves from her body toward Seth.

How horrible! Nefertiti is sacrificing her soul to erase Pollione's disfigurement.

"No, no, my queen!" I cry.

I leap between Nefertiti and Seth, colliding with her soul. The light engulfs me. I feel I'm being consumed by fire.

I have her soul!

Seth's voice explodes like thunder, making the ground shake and me as well. "Accursed cat! Who are you?"

"I am Pollione."

"But you are a cat!"

"Oh, Tati . . ." Nefertiti cries, collapsing.

Seth's laughter is even more menacing than his anger. "What a fool," he says, nodding towards the unconscious queen. Then bowing his asinine head to me, he adds, "You are a bigger trickster than I am!"

He's right. I am a trickster, and the realization horrifies me.

Seth grows taller and taller, then disappears back into thin air. I rush to Nefertiti and rub my face against hers. She's breathing very softly, as if she were sleeping. How vulnerable she appears, the locks of her wig upturned like the wings of a dead bird.

Memories of our shared moments flow over me like the inundating waters of the Nile, drowning me in a feeling I've never felt before, not for the High Priest or Elena, not even for the Pharaoh.

I loved Nefertiti. Now I am in love with her.

I fear it, yet welcome it.

What's happening to me? I must go back to Maru-Aten and tell the High Priest what took place here!

"I promise, my queen," I whisper in Nefertiti's ear, "I'll be back never to leave your side again."

I run down the path and past the queen's chariot. The horses' neighs are like the wails of grieving women. They echo in my mind throughout my journey back to Maru-Aten.

Chapter 28

I wake up from a deep sleep. The room I see is a far cry from the luxurious surroundings I've gotten used to lately. The only furniture is the bed I'm lying in and a small table next to it with a jar and a bowl. There's a lit oil lamp on the table casting my shadow on a wall that's white-washed instead of richly painted.

Someone enters the room. It's the High Priest!

"Finally," he says. "You gave me quite a fright, Wrappa-Hamen . . . Here. Drink some water."

He lifts the jar from the table, pours water into the bowl, and brings the bowl to my lips. I lap it all up.

"Are you well enough now to speak?"

"Are these your quarters? How did I get here?"

"Yes, you are in my quarters. As the night patrol was making its rounds, one of the guards found you bleeding and unconscious just outside the walls. When I first arrived at Maru-Aten, I cured an infection for him with honey and herbs from the gardens here. He thought I could help you too."

"You said I was bleeding."

"Look at your paws. They are raw."

From my trek back to Maru-Aten!

"They don't hurt much."

"I applied a paste made of honey and coriander seeds to sooth them. Do you remember what happened?"

"Yes."

"You were with Nefertiti?"

"Yes!"

"You saw what happened to her?"

"Worse. I caused it!" I tell him everything.

"Yes, the Lovers, the fifth Tarot card in my reading. Seth was the evil force you had to face in your distant future—"

"Please, no time for that now," I cry. "We've wasted enough time as it is. We must go to the hills to Nefertiti."

I try getting up from the bed, but fall back on it.

"We will, we will. But first let me give you some wine. It will restore you." He leaves the room and comes back a moment later holding a humble wine goblet. "You will feel better soon," he says,

187

putting the goblet to my mouth.

The wine tastes so bitter I stop drinking after a few laps.

"Drink all of it!"

I do as I'm told . . . The room expands and contracts . . . Nefertiti is riding in her chariot . . . The frogs are dancing around the pond . . . Heket has me in the pool . . . I'm flying over Maru-Aten . . . I'm falling . . . falling.

"Whaat diid youu puut . . . wiiine?" I manage to say just before my spinning head collapses on my chest . . .

Someone is shaking me. I open my eyes, meet the scrutinizing gaze of the High Priest—and smell the musty odor of the attic in Bath!

"You took us back," I cry, alarmed. "We left Nefertiti! What did you put in the wine?"

"Mandrake."

"Mandrake! No wonder I was hallucinating. You maniac!"

"Mmm, it was meant to make you sleep, but I might have used a pinch too much. I was in a hurry. The Tarot card that stood for the obstacles you would face was the Hermit. Time. Time was against you. You had begun to change."

"What do you mean?"

"Look at yourself."

When I raise a foreleg, I don't believe my eyes. I run from the cabin, jump off the boat, and go to the mirror in a corner of the attic, half covered by a sheet. I pull the sheet away and behold a naked man. Tall, middle aged, heavy set, with lapis-blue eyes, a Roman nose, long thin lips, and a crown of dark silver hair.

"You were a beautiful cat," the High Priest says, "and now you are a handsome man, even with the excess flesh. You are taller than I am, but then you were a bruiser."

My eyesight is not as sharp as it was. I have to move closer to the mirror to see my reflection clearly. I still have the star on my forehead and beside it a faint scar.

For the love of the gods, so much has happened between now and the day I hurt myself on the windowsill back in New York!

The High Priest takes hold of my arm and guides me to the nearest chair.

"I'm still hallucinating, right?" I say, collapsing into it.

"No, Wrappa-Hamen, it is true. Nefertiti's soul did more than just imbue your love for her with passion. It transformed you physically as well . . . But you must return Nefertiti's soul."

"Why? I love her. Now that I'm a man we can be together."

"I believe the reason for Nefertiti's immortality is the loss of her soul. You must return it to her so she can die. And soon! Or her soul will become inseparable from yours, like ivy taking root on a brick wall."

Nanette's prophecy's to Nefertiti—"Neither man nor beast will set you free, but the hybrid in between"—has come to pass. But she didn't mean the hybrid I was, a cat with human characteristics. She meant the hybrid I was to become. A man with both a human and a feline soul.

"How can I allow the woman I love to die?" I ask.

"Wrappa-Hamen, now we know the terrible choice predicted by the Lovers was between Nefertiti's life and her death. The Tarot card Strength stood for the influences in your favor. It is your inner strength that will enable you to do what you must."

"When I give her soul back, will I be a cat again?"

"Yes, you will be a cat again. But as was also predicted by Strength, 'Your old self you will shed to become him again and yet new.'"

"I don't understand."

The High Priest smiles ruefully. "You will always have the memory of what you felt for Nefertiti when you were a man. Remember the stanza I recited to you?

I am the One that transforms into Two.
I am Two that transforms into Four.
I am Four that transforms into Eight.
After this I am One.

It is an ancient stanza alluding to the mystery of creation. When you are a cat again, you will be even more human than before. You will be a new creation."

His words fail to console me, and I begin to cry uncontrollably.

"Shouldn't you have told me to give Nefertiti her soul back when we were still in ancient Egypt?" I ask between one sob and another. "Then she would've died when her time came. It would have spared her thousands of years of loneliness and pain."

The High Priest kneels by my side. "My dear friend, don't you see?" he says, putting a hand on my shoulder. "Nefertiti was already here in Bath. Her past could not be changed. What has taken place is unalterable. All one can do is shape the present. You can end Nefertiti's misery . . . She's waiting for you."

"You've talked to her?"

"Yes. I have told her what happened. But she does not remember."

"Then if she doesn't remember me, she doesn't love me."

"I am sorry. Perhaps when she is whole again . . ."

"How do I return her soul?"

"The way Seth told Nefertiti to surrender it. Will it away."

"How long do we have together after that?"

"It can be only moments, Wrappa-Hamen."

The High Priest gives me his robe to wear, and I make my way down to Nefertiti's secret chamber, shaking with terror. I feel I have no inner strength left!

When the High Priest interpreted the Lovers, he failed to see I'd fall in love. Any other time it would give me great satisfaction to call him an ignoramus, but not today. No, not today.

I enter Nefertiti's secret chamber and bolt the door behind me. No one will leave or enter this tomb again. She's lighting incense in the burner. Her back is to me. I call her name.

"Pollione?" she says, turning slowly.

I rush over to her and struggle against the desire to take her in my arms.

Death will not be disappointed. Her face is perfectly made up, as if Tia had done it. Her hair is loose, thick, and shiny with perfumed oil. Her long linen tunic envelopes her body as tightly as the linen strips on a mummy, revealing her sinuous form in all its beauty.

My heart is racing.

She caresses my face with her right hand. On her little finger

190

is the only piece of jewelry she's wearing today. The gold ring.

Dare I hope she remembers?

"Your ring . . ."

"I do not know why," she says as she takes her hand away, "but I could never part with it. Today I will have to . . ."

My heart is breaking.

"Gato-Hamen told me we loved each other once," she says. "For the sake of that love, act now. Kiss me. Kill me with your kiss."

Her words are a command, but I hesitate.

"Kiss me, Pollione!" she insists. "Time is against us."

I put a hand on her lips. Hearing what I must do from the High Priest was painful enough. Hearing it from her nearly sends me to my knees.

But when she dies, I want to be standing! I take her in my arms and hold her tight, hoping death will take me too.

We kiss. I feel as if a mighty hand were tearing my chest apart. The pain forces me to let go of her.

A pulsating white light leaves my body and briefly hovers between us, before she and it become one.

"I remember everything from the moment you sang in the tomb," she cries. "I remember you cried out to me and I realized Pollione was Tati. I saw you leap between me and Seth. I saw my soul enter you. I heard Seth's anger. It shook the hills. Whether cat or man I loved you. I loved your soul. I collapsed believing Seth was going to kill you. It was more than I could bear . . ."

I take her back in my arms. She leans on me, unable to stand on her own any longer.

"I regained consciousness not knowing why I was there . . . In a daze, I made my way down from the cliffs and found my chariot waiting for me. The horses knew their way back to the city . . . I woke up in the morning . . . "

"Oh, my beloved queen, forgive me," I beg. "If I hadn't tricked you into believing I was a disfigured man—"

"It was Seth who tricked me! When he told me he wanted my soul in exchange for erasing your disfigurement, he said the loss of my soul only meant I would not have an afterlife. I thought, better a few years with you, than eternal life in the other world. Seth neglected to tell me that a body with no soul never dies. Although my soul went to you instead of Seth, the result was the same. I was going to live for ever. But then I met Nanette . . . You ask me to forgive you, but there is nothing to forgive."

We kiss again. Then, smiling ruefully, she runs her fingers over the star and the scar on my brow.

"You are the beginning and the end of a dream," she says. "Our love would never be understood by this world. We had only moments. We have now. For that, I would give up my soul again."

Under the makeup, her face is pallid. The light in her eyes is fading.

"Recite your poem," she says in a whisper.

"No longer are the stars in the sky . . ."

Nefertiti body has turned cold.

"No longer is a man's heart his . . ."

She is turning to dust in my arms.

"Thou, my queen, have captured all."

The dust flows to the ground like sand in an hour glass. I remain standing, clutching my forelegs to my chest until, exhausted, I fall down and curl up beside it.

Elena and the High Priest have been begging me for days to unbolt the door. By now, just as I no longer feel hunger or thirst, I barely hear them. My vision too is all but gone. But in my heart I hear Nefertiti's voice clearly and see her face, the face of the most beautiful woman a cat or man could ever behold.

The sixth card of the tarot reading, which went unread, the card revealing the final outcome—surely it was Death. I feel my spirit leaving my body . . .

"Wapamen, opun. Opun, Wapamen."

My Pharaoh has commanded me!

I drag myself over to the door, and with strength given to me by the great love behind it, I stand and push the bolt back.

I am and always will be the Pharaoh's cat.

Chapter 29

It's what Elena calls a glorious day. The sky is clear blue with some big white floating clouds. She and the High Priest are walking down a road leading to the cemetery gate. She's carrying the little Pharaoh. He's carrying a rolled-up blanket, a large basket, and me in the pet carrier bag.

The gate is ajar. Elena pushes it open, and we enter. On the left side is a cottage. "This is the caretaker's home," she says.

She knocks on the door. No answer.

"I wonder if Bill still lives here. He was an old man when I knew him. Maybe he now dwells in another part of the cemetery."

The High Priest opens the door of the carrier bag. I jump out, but stay on all fours, just in case someone should come by.

The cemetery seems a playing field where sun and shade compete. Some graves lie in bright sunlight, others in the long shadows of cypress trees. The only sounds are the birds chirping and the crunch of our steps on the gravel. There's a smell of burning leaves in the air.

I feel at peace here and imagine that Nefertiti too is at peace.

The graves are encircled by tall verdant grass speckled with wild flowers. As we move among the graves, Elena explains that some are more than two hundred years old.

She leads us up a hill to a red granite column, which she says is a Victorian monument. It looks about four feet tall. Inlaid in its swirls are bits of colored glass. There are many gaps left by the bits that have fallen out over the years.

"When I was a child," Elena says ruefully as she pushes a loose blue bit back into place with the index finger of her free hand, "I believed that these were precious jewels."

As she turns to leave, the blue bit falls out.

We go down the hill and turn onto a path that forks. Elena goes left. The High Priest and I follow her.

"This is the spot," she says after a few minutes, "where my parents and I would have our picnic."

On the spot stands a tall full cypress tree. "Oh, my friend, how you have grown!"

The tree sways in the wind. If it could talk, I believe it would say, "You've grown too, little Elena. It's been so long since I last saw you that I hardly recognize you. You're quite a lady now. Is this strange group your family?"

Elena rests a hand on the trunk of the tree. She's lost in thought.

The High Priest takes a kerchief out of his pocket and gently wipes the tears from her face.

"We had such a good time here, my parents and I."

"Now you will have a good time with us."

"Gato-Hamen, you always know the right thing to say."

Always? I disagree, but keep it to myself.

"Let's begin our good time then," Elena says, her voice joyful.

Holding the little Pharaoh in one arm, she uses the other to take the rolled-up blanket from the High Priest. He puts down the basket and the carrier bag and helps her spread the blanket on the grass. She puts the little Pharaoh on the blanket and sets the basket in the middle.

"Let's all sit."

When we've settled, she opens the basket. The delicious aroma makes me salivate. John has prepared our picnic, and if there's something he excels at, it's preparing delicious meals.

Elena takes out three multicolored paper plates and three sets of plastic cutlery and puts them on the blanket. Next she takes out small sandwiches—ham and pickles, boiled eggs and watercress, smoked salmon and butter—long with a whole roast chicken and small packages of potato chips. When I think the basket is empty, she takes out a tray containing an assortment of cheeses—blue, white, yellow—surrounded by grapes.

Now I'm salivating uncontrollably. I stretch my forepaws toward the chicken, but Elena is faster and puts her hand in front of my paws. "First, we're having a toast. You must keep your palate clean."

With all the salivating I've been doing, my palate couldn't be cleaner!

As if handling a sacred object, she takes a bundle of tissue paper out of the basket and unwraps three glasses. "These were Nefertiti's. They're old Venetian Glasses, from a service of twenty four."

In the same careful manner, she takes a container out the basket and opens the lid. She removes a bottle of wine, wet from the ice, and hands to the High Priest.

He pushes under the cork, which is fat and round, with his thumbs. After he struggles for several seconds, the cork shoots out with a loud pop and flies between my ears. I quickly turn around to see it hit a gravestone.

I recall an incident thousands of years ago in Egypt when the Pharaoh and I were jumping up and own on a mattress made of a hippo skin filled with air. The cork popped out of the hippo's ass and hit the Vizier on the forehead . . .

I'm relishing the memory when Elena's cry brings me back, or forward, to the present. "Quick, quick, pour it in the glasses!"

Foaming white wine is coming out of the bottle.

"I've never seen wine like this before," I say.

"It's champagne. Bollinger, Grande Annee 1990. Nefertiti had quite a few bottles of it in her wine cellar."

As Elena pours milk into a small mug for the little Pharaoh and hands it to him, the High Priest manages to pour the champagne into the glasses. Only a little spills on the blanket.

He, Elena, and I each take a glass. "To the memory of Nefertiti," says Elena raising her glass.

The High Priest and I raise our glasses. The little Pharaoh -raises his mug. We all tap our glasses against his mug. He giggles.

"To Nefertiti," we say in unison. The little Pharaoh giggles again.

I take a sip of the bubbling liquid. Mmm. I take another sip, then another. The bubbles travel up my nose and explode in my head. I sip and sip till my glass is empty.

"Let's have another glass, old chap," I tell the High Priest, who quickly obliges.

Elena gives me a chicken wing. It's salty, just the way I like it. And this liquid gold goes so well with it. Very well indeed.

Ah, this is the life. Good food, good drink, good company, and a beautiful bucolic view—the cottage with its red tile roof, a pond, and a field where a large reddish-brown horse and a gray donkey are grazing.

The sandwiches are delicious, especially the smoked salmon. But all this salty food has made me thirsty. The bottle is nearby. I pour myself another glass. Heavens, this stuff is delicious. I begin to hiccup.

"Wrappa-Hamen," Elena asks, "you aren't drunk, are you?"

"Drunk, drunk, you zay?" I reply, raising my glass. "Jussst a bit, bitsy inebrrriated."

Elena shakes her head. I wish she wouldn't do that. It's making me dizzy. She's also shaking a finger at me, or is it two fingers? She mumbles something that sounds like, "I have two babies, not one."

The High Priest doesn't look like a baby. Sometimes Elena makes no sense. The last thing I remember before passing out is tepid coffee being poured down my throat . . .

When I wake up my head hurts. It feels as if someone has hit it. Looking at the sun's position in the sky, I guess I've slept a couple of hours. Elena and the High Priest are sleeping with the little Pharaoh nestled between them, contentedly, with his thumb in his mouth.

Nefertiti's glass eye hangs from a gold chain around Elena's neck. I coughed it up some time ago, along with a fur ball, and asked John to make it into a pendant for her.

I'm reminiscing about the day I swallowed the eye when I hear the rustle of leaves coming from behind the bushes at the far end of the cemetery. A small doe breaks through the bushes and looks at me. When I get up, she runs away. She's agile and light. She runs around or jumps over the gravestones in her way.

I follow her. Stuffed and hung-over, I'm slow and clumsy. The doe stops, as if waiting for me to catch up. I move closer. When I'm close enough to see her dark liquid eyes and twitching nose, off she goes.

Chasing her, I've entered a part of the cemetery completely surrounded by trees. The branches have created a cupola. There's no grass on the ground, only a carpet of dead leaves. It's dark in here. The graves are hard to see.

The only light is a single sunbeam stealing through the thick branches. It falls upon a sarcophagus. Like all the others, it's almost completely covered by ivy and other vine plants.

I walk over to it and pull the ivy away from the spot the sunbeam has lit up.

In Memoriam
Nefertiti
1370 BC 2015 AD

I let go of the ivy, and the engraving is covered again. "Farewell, my queen, farewell," I say as I leave the sacred place to return to my family.

The lightest drizzle has begun to fall. I stop in front of a statue of a young woman, the white of the stone stained by the moss growing over it. The young woman is looking skyward. Her hair falls in waves to her shoulders. Her arms are crossed on her chest, like a mummy. Her robe covers her entire body, its heavy folds gathered about her bare feet.

I see the pond in the distance. The raindrops create small circles as they hit the water. The horse and the donkey are being lead to the stable. Farther away, on the hills, are the houses of Bathwick half hidden by the trees. Even farther, to the left, the city of Bath nestles in a valley and reaches up into the steep hills.

The rain seems to have intensified all the colors—the greens of the fields and the trees, the red tiles on the cottage roofs, the various shades of the stones.

It's also made the setting melancholy. But, still, I want to stand here under the rain and look on it forever.

"Wrappa-Hamen!" It's Elena.

I turn and see the familiar trio. She's lugging the carrier bag and the food basket. The High Priest is carrying the little Pharaoh in his arms. The picnic blanket is over their heads.

"We'd better get going," Elena warns. "It looks as though it might begin to pour any minute . . . Typical English weather."

She puts the carrier bag down and points to a man in the field. "Is that old Bill?"

She raises her hand as if she's about to call to him. But she doesn't.

"Are you not going to see if it is Bill?" the High Priest asks when she puts her hand down.

She shakes her head as she picks up the carrier bag. She's thinking that the man might be Bill, but then he might not be. She'd rather be in doubt than risk finding out he's gone.

I can read her thoughts because I'm thinking along the same lines. I'm afraid that if I take her and the High Priest to Nefertiti's grave, it won't be there. I don't want to risk discovering that is was only a drunken hallucination and have Elena lecture me on the dangers of drinking too much.

She and I keep our doubts to ourselves as we leave the cemetery and she pulls the gate closed.

About the Author

Maria Luisa Lang has published two novels, *The Pharaoh's Cat* and *The Eye of Nefertiti*, which is both a sequel to *The Pharaoh's Cat* and a stand-alone novel. She was born in Rome, Italy, and lives in New York City. She often returns to Italy to visit her family and has stayed for extended periods in Bath and London. She has a degree in art from the City University of New York, and her artwork has been exhibited in New York galleries. She is an amateur Egyptologist. Her love of cats and ancient Egypt has inspired her to write two novels set there with a very special cat as her protagonist. Both *The Pharaoh's Cat* and *The Eye of Nefertiti* are available on Amazon in paperback and in a Kindle edition.

Printed in Great Britain
by Amazon